Sir Arthur Conan Doyle's
THE ADVENTURES OF
SHERLOCK HOLMES

Sir Arthur Conan Doyle's

THE ADVENTURES OF
SHERLOCK HOLMES

BOOK TWO

The Sign of The Four
The Adventure of the Blue Carbuncle
The Adventure of the Speckled Band

Adapted for young readers by
CATHERINE EDWARDS SADLER

Illustrated by ANDREW GLASS

AN AVON CAMELOT BOOK

SIR ARTHUR CONAN DOYLE'S
THE ADVENTURES OF SHERLOCK HOLMES
adapted by Catherine Edwards Sadler
is an original publication of Avon Books.
This work has never before
appeared in book form.

AVON BOOKS
A division of
The Hearst Corporation
959 Eighth Avenue
New York, New York 10019

First Camelot Printing, November, 1981

Sadler, Catherine Edwards.
  Sir Arthur Conan Doyle's The Adventures of Sherlock Holmes.

  (An Avon Camelot book)
  Contents: Bk. 1. A study in scarlet. The red-headed league. The man
with the twisted lip — Bk. 2. The sign of the four. The adventure of the
blue carbuncle. The adventure of the speckled band — Bk. 3. The
adventure of the engineer's thumb. The adventure of the beryl
coronet. The adventure of silver blaze. The adventure of the Musgrave
ritual — [etc.]
  1. Detective and mystery stories, American.
2. Children's stories, American. [1. Mystery and detective stories.
2. Short stories] I. Glass, Andrew, ill.

II. Doyle, Arthur Conan, Sir, 1859-1930. Adventures of Sherlock
Holmes. III. Title. IV. Title: Adventures of Sherlock Holmes.
PZ7.S1238Si   [Fic]   81-65084
                         AACR2

Table of Contents

Introduction

Sir Arthur Conan Doyle was born in Edinburgh, Scotland, on May 22, 1859. In 1876 he entered the Edinburgh Medical College as a student of medicine. There he met a certain professor named Joseph Bell. Bell enjoyed amusing his students in a most unusual way. He would tell them a patient's medical and personal history before the patient had uttered a single word! He would observe the exact appearance of the patient and note the smallest detail about him: marks on his hands, stains on his clothing, the jewelry he wore. He would observe a tattoo, a new gold chain, a worn hat with unusual stains upon it. From these *observations* he would then make *deductions.* In other words, he would come to conclusions by reasoning in a logical manner. For example, a tattoo and the way a man walked could lead to the deduction that the man had been to sea; a new gold chain could lead to the deduction that he had come into recent wealth. Time and time again Professor Bell's deductions proved correct!

Conan Doyle was intrigued by Professor Bell's skills of observation and deduction. Since his early youth he had been fascinated by the mysterious. He loved mysteries and detective stories. He himself had already tried his hand at writing. Now a new sort of hero began to take shape in Conan Doyle's mind. His hero would be a detective—not just an ordinary detective, though. No, he would be extraordinary...a man like Bell who observed the smallest detail. He would take his skills of observation and work them out to an exact science—the science of deduction. "It is all very well to say that a man is clever," Conan Doyle wrote, "but the reader wants to see examples of it—such examples as Bell gave us every day...." So Conan Doyle created just such a clever man, a man who had perfected the skill of observation, turned it into an exact science, and then used it as the basis of his career. His cleverness would be revealed in the extraordinary methods he used to solve his cases and capture his criminals.

Little by little the personality and world of his new character took shape. At last he became the sharp-featured fellow we all know as Mr. Sherlock Holmes. Next Conan Doyle turned his imagination to Holmes' surroundings—those "comfortable rooms in Baker Street"—where the fire was always blazing and where footsteps were always heard on the stair. And then there was Watson, dear old Watson! He was much like Conan Doyle himself, easygoing, typically British, a doctor and a writer. Watson would be Holmes' sidekick, his friend and his chronicler. He would be humble and admiring, always asking Holmes to explain his theories, always ready to go out into the foggy, gaslit streets of London on some mysterious mission. All that remained to create were the adventures themselves.

Taking up his pen in 1886, Conan Doyle set to work on a short novel, or novella as it is sometimes called. He finished *A Study in Scarlet* in just two months. It was the first of sixty Sherlock Holmes stories to come and it began a career for Dr. Arthur Conan Doyle that would eventually win him a knighthood.

Today Holmes is considered one of—if not *the*—most popular fictional heroes of all time. More has been written about this character than any other. Sherlock Holmes societies have been created, plays and movies based on the detective have been made, a castle in Switzerland houses a Sherlock Holmes collection, a tavern in London bears his name and features a reconstruction of his rooms in Baker Street. He has even been poked fun at and been called everything from Picklock Holes to Hemlock Jones!

Why such a fuss over a character who appeared in a series of stories close to a century ago? Elementary, dear reader! He is loved. He is loved for his genius, his coolness, his individuality, and for the safety he represents. For as long as Sherlock Holmes is alive the world is somehow safe. The villains will be outsmarted and good and justice will win out. And so he has been kept alive these hundred years by readers around the globe. And since today we are still in need of just such a clever hero it seems a safe deduction that Mr. Sherlock Holmes—and his dear old Watson—will go on living in these pages for a good many more years to come.

The
Sign
of
the
Four

Like *A Study in Scarlet, The Sign of the Four* was not an immediate success. Perhaps the public was just not ready for Sherlock Holmes, or perhaps the length of the novellas put readers off. Whatever the reason, it was not until Conan Doyle came up with the idea of putting Holmes into a series of short stories that he was "discovered."

The Sign of the Four actually contains a number of mysteries: the curious disappearance of Captain Morstan, the bizarre murder of Bartholomew Sholto, the hidden meaning of the sign of the four and the whereabouts of the villain Small and the Agra treasure. The cast of characters is indeed unusual: a wooden-legged convict and his pygmy mate, the red-headed twins, a pair of prizefighters, Indian servants, and a gentle, wronged girl. Together they move through this fast-paced tale which Conan Doyle considered one of his best.

Chapter 1
The Science of Deduction

In our years together as roommates, there were many times when Mr. Sherlock Holmes' actions upset me. There were times, for instance, when he would lounge about for days on end. He would not even bother to dress or eat. It was after one such period that I scolded him for taking such poor care of himself.

"My mind," he said in defense, "rebels at boredom. Give me the most complex theory to work out. That is when I am happy. But when I have no work I feel lifeless. I hate the dull routine of everyday life. I crave mental work. That is why I have chosen my profession . . . or, rather, why I have created it. For I am the only one in the world."

"The only unofficial detective?" I asked.

"The only unofficial consulting detective," he answered. "People come to me when all else has failed. I am the last court of appeal. They look to me when the police have given up or cannot find a clue. Sometimes the police themselves lay a case before me. Only this morning I received a letter from the famous French detective, Francois Le Villard. He wishes my assistance on a case."

Holmes tossed over a crumpled sheet of notepaper. I glanced at it. It was full of praise for Holmes' past victories.

"He rates my assistance too highly," said Sherlock Holmes. "He is a very fine detective himself. He possesses two of the three traits necessary for an ideal detective. He has the power of observation and the power of deduction. All he lacks is the knowledge of small detail. But that will come in time. He is now translating my small works into French."

"Your works?"

"Oh, you didn't know?" Holmes asked. "Yes, I have written several small pamphlets. They are all on technical subjects. One, for example, explains the differences between cigarette, cigar, and pipe tobacco ash. Such information can be of great use to the detective. If you know that a murder was done by a man who smokes an Indian cigar, you are much closer to finding your suspect."

"You have an extraordinary genius for detail," said I.

"I appreciate its importance. I have also written on footprints and how a person's hand reveals his work. But you are weary of my hobby."

"Not at all," I answered. "It is of the greatest interest to me. You spoke just now of observation and deduction. Surely they are the same thing."

"Why, hardly," said Holmes. "For example, observation shows me that you have been to the post office this morning. But deduction tells me that you sent a telegram rather than a letter."

"Right!" said I. "Right on both points! But I don't see how you figured it out. I did it on the spur of the moment and told no one."

"It is simplicity itself," remarked Sherlock Holmes.

"I observed a little reddish earth on the sole of your shoe. Just opposite the post office, they have taken up the pavement. They have dug up the earth and dumped it to the side. It is difficult to avoid stepping on it when entering the post office. The earth is of a peculiar reddish tint found nowhere else in the neighborhood. So much for observation. The rest is deduction."

"How, then, did you deduce the telegram?" I asked.

"Why, I knew that you hadn't written a letter. I sat opposite you all morning and you did not write one. You have a sheet of stamps and a thick bundle of postcards in your desk. Why, then, would you go to a post office except to send a wire? Eliminate all other possibilities, and one is left with the truth."

"In this case it certainly is so," I replied. "May I put you to a harder test?"

"I should be delighted," he replied.

"I have heard you say that you can tell a man's character from the objects he owns. Now, I have here a watch. It was recently sent to me. Can you tell me the character or habits of the late owner?"

I handed him the watch. I felt quite amused as I knew it was an impossible test. He balanced the watch in his hand. He gazed hard at the dial and then opened the back. First he examined the works with his eyes and then with a magnifying glass. Finally he snapped shut the case and handed it back.

"There is little information," he remarked. "The watch has been recently cleaned. This robs me of many important facts."

"You are right," I answered. "It was cleaned before being sent to me." In my heart I accused Holmes of giving me an excuse to cover his failure. What information could he expect to learn from a watch?

"My research, however, has not been a total failure," he said. "I should judge that the watch belonged to your elder brother, who inherited it from your father."

"That you gather, no doubt, from the H.W. upon the back?"

"Quite so. The W. suggests your own last name. The date of the watch is nearly fifty years back. The initials are as old as the watch, so it was made for the last generation. Jewelry is usually handed down to the eldest son, who is most likely to have the same first name. If I remember right, your father has been dead many years. It has, therefore, been in the hands of your eldest brother."

"Right so far," said I. "Anything else?"

"He was a man of untidy habits—very untidy and careless. Your father's death left him well-off, but he wasted his money. He lived for some time in poverty although he did prosper from time to time. Finally he took to drink and died. This is all I can gather."

I sprang from my chair. I paced about the room with bitterness in my heart.

"This is unworthy of you, Holmes!" I said. "I cannot believe that you have sunk so low. You have clearly learned about my unhappy brother. And now you pretend to deduce this knowledge to prove your theory. You cannot expect me to believe that you have read all this from his old watch."

"My dear Doctor," said he. "Please accept my apologies. I was looking at the matter simply as a problem to solve. I had forgotten how personal and painful it might be to you. I assure you, however, that I never even knew you had a brother until you handed me the watch."

"Then how did you get these facts? They are absolutely correct in every way," I said.

"Ah, that is good luck. I could only say what seemed probable. I did not expect to be so accurate."

"But it wasn't mere guesswork?"

"No, no. I never guess. It is a shocking habit. It seems strange to you because you do not follow my train of thought. For example, I began by stating that your brother was careless. Look at the lower part of the watchcase. It is dented in two places. It is cut and marked all over. That is from keeping other hard objects, such as coins and keys, in the same pocket. A man who treats so good a watch in such a way is clearly careless. And a man who inherits so fine a watch usually inherits much more."

I nodded to show that I followed his reasoning.

Holmes continued, "English pawnbrokers scratch the ticket number upon the inside of the case. This is more handy than a label and there is no risk of the number being lost or mixed-up. There are no less than four such numbers on the inside of this case. First deduction: that your brother had his share of hard times. Second deduction: that he also had better times—or else he couldn't have reclaimed his watch. Finally, I ask you to look at the key hole. Look at the thousands of scratches all round the hole. These are marks where the key has slipped. What sober man's key could have made such marks? But you will never find a drunkard's watch without them. He winds it at night and leaves these traces of his unsteady hand. Where is the mystery in all this?"

"It is clear as daylight," I answered. "I regret my outburst. I should have had more faith in your marvelous skill. May I ask whether you are working on a case at present?"

"None. That is why I have been so bored of late. I cannot live without brainwork. What else is there to live for? What is the use of having powers when one has no use for them?"

I was about to reply when there was a crisp knock at the door. Our landlady entered. She carried a card on a small silver tray.

"A young lady is here to see you, sir," she said to Holmes.

"Miss Mary Morstan," he read. "Hum! I have no recollection of that name. Ask the young lady to step up, Mrs. Hudson. Don't go, Doctor. I should prefer you to remain."

Chapter 2
The Statement of the Case

Miss Morstan entered the room with a firm step. She was small, dainty, and simply dressed. Her expression was sweet and friendly and her large blue eyes were striking. Holmes offered her a seat. As she took it, her lip trembled and her hand quivered in intense emotion.

"I have come to you, Mr. Holmes," she said, "because you once helped my employer, Mrs. Cecil Forrester. She was much impressed by your kindness and skill."

"Mrs. Cecil Forrester," he repeated thoughtfully. "I believe I was of some slight service to her. The case, however, was a very simple one."

"She did not think so. But at least you cannot say the same of mine. I can hardly imagine anything more strange," Miss Morstan said.

Holmes rubbed his hands and his eyes glistened. He leaned forward in his chair. "State your case," said he in a businesslike way.

"Briefly," she said, "the facts are these. My father was an officer in an Indian regiment. He sent me back to England when I was quite small. My mother was dead, and I had no relative in England. I was placed in a boarding school in Edinburgh. I remained there until I was seventeen years of age. In the year 1878 my father obtained twelve months leave and came home. He telegraphed me from London that he had arrived safely. He directed me to come down at once. He gave the Langham Hotel as his address. His message was full of kindness and love. On reaching London, I drove to the Langham. I was informed that Captain Morstan was staying there, but he had gone out the night before and had not returned. I waited all day without news of him. That night I contacted the police. The next morning we advertised in all the papers. Our inquiries led to no result. From that day to this no word has ever been heard of my unfortunate father. He came home with his heart full of hope to find some peace, some new comfort and instead—" She put her hand to her throat. A choking sob cut short her sentence.

"The date?" asked Holmes.

"He disappeared on the 3rd of December, 1878—nearly ten years ago."

"His luggage?"

"Remained at the hotel. There was nothing in it to suggest a clue—some clothes, some books, and a large number of curiosities from the Andaman Islands, which belong to India, as you may know. He had been one of the officers in charge of a prison camp there."

"Had he any friends here in London?" asked Holmes.

"Only one that I know of—Major Sholto. He belonged to the same regiment. The Major had retired some time before and moved to the London suburb of Upper Norwood. We communicated with him, of course. He did not even know that his friend was in England."

"An unusual case," remarked Holmes.

"I have not described to you the most unusual part.

About six years ago—to be exact, upon the 4th of May 1882—an advertisement appeared in the *Times*. It asked for the address of Miss Mary Morstan. It stated that it would be to her advantage to come forward. There was no name or address to contact. I had already begun to work for Mrs. Cecil Forrester as a governess. At her advice I published my address in the advertisement column. The next day I received a small cardboard box. In it I found a very large and lustrous pearl. No note was enclosed. I have received a similar box every year upon that date. Each one has contained a pearl. An expert has stated that they are very rare and of great value. You can see for yourselves."

She opened a flat box as she spoke. She showed me six of the finest pearls that I had ever seen.

"Your statement is most interesting," said Sherlock Holmes. "Has anything else occurred to you?"

"Yes, and no later than today. That is why I have come to you. This morning I received this letter. Perhaps you will read it for yourself."

"Thank you," said Holmes. "The envelope too, please. Postmark: London. Date: July 7. Hum! Man's thumb-mark on the corner—probably postman. Best quality paper. Expensive envelope. No address. 'BE AT THE THIRD PILLAR FROM THE LEFT OUTSIDE THE LYCEUM THEATRE TONIGHT AT SEVEN O'CLOCK. IF YOU ARE DIS-TRUSTFUL, BRING TWO FRIENDS. YOU ARE A WRONGED WOMAN. YOU SHALL HAVE JUSTICE. DO NOT BRING POLICE. IF YOU DO, ALL WILL BE FOR NOTHING. YOUR UNKNOWN FRIEND.' Well, really, this is a very pretty little mystery. What do you intend to do, Miss Morstan?"

"That is exactly what I want to ask you," she said.

"Then we shall most certainly go. You and I and—yes, why, Dr. Watson is the very man. The letter says to bring two friends. He and I have worked together before."

"But would he come?" she asked.

"I should be proud and happy to be of service," said I.

"You are both very kind," she answered. "I have led a lonely life and have no friends to go to. If I am here at six, will it do?"

"You must not be later," said Holmes. "There is one other point, however. Was the handwriting on the box addresses the same as in this letter?"

"I have them here," she answered. She produced half a dozen pieces of paper.

"You are certainly a model client. Let us see, now." He spread out the papers on the table. His eyes darted back and forth between them. "There can be no question about it. They were undoubtedly written by the same person. I do not want to give you false hope, Miss Morstan. But is there any resemblance between this handwriting and that of your father?"

"Nothing could be more unlike," she said.

"I expected you to say that! We shall look for you at six. Please allow me to keep the papers. I may look into the matter before then. It is only half-past three. Goodbye."

"Goodbye," said our visitor. She glanced at both of us in a kindly manner. Then she replaced her pearl-box and hurried away.

"What a beautiful woman," I said admiringly.

"What an interesting case," replied Sherlock Holmes.

Chapter 3
In Quest of a Solution

It was half-past five before Holmes returned from his afternoon outing. He was bright, eager, and in excellent spirits.

"There is no great mystery in this matter," he said. "The facts appear to lead to only one explanation."

"What! You have solved it already?" I asked.

"Well, that would be too much to say. I have discovered an important fact. The details are still to be added. I have just consulted the back files of the *Times*. It turns out that Major Sholto died upon the 28th of April, 1882."

"I fail to see what that suggests," said I.

"No? You surprise me. Look at it this way, then. Captain Morstan disappears. The only person in London whom he could have visited is Major Sholto. Major Sholto denies having heard that Morstan was in London. Four years later Sholto dies. *Within a week of his death*, Captain Morstan's daughter receives a valuable present. This is repeated year after year. It now ends with a letter which describes her as a wronged woman. What wrong can it mean? Only that she has been deprived a father? And why should the presents begin immediately after Sholto's death?—unless Sholto's heir knows something of the mystery and is trying to repay her somehow? Have you another theory to meet all the facts?"

"But what a strange way of making it up to her! And why does he write to her now, rather than six years ago? Again, the letter speaks of giving her justice. What justice can she have? It is too much to hope that her father is still alive."

"There are certainly a number of questions still to answer in the case," said Sherlock Holmes. "But our expedition tonight will solve it all. Ah, here is a cab and Miss Morstan is inside. Are you ready? Then we had better go down, for it is a little past the hour."

I picked up my hat and my heaviest stick. Holmes meanwhile took his revolver from the drawer and slipped it into his pocket. It was clear that he thought our night's work dangerous.

Miss Morstan was muffled in a dark cloak and her face was pale. She must have been uneasy about the strange adventure we were on, but she answered Sherlock's questions calmly.

"Major Sholto was a very particular friend of Papa's," she said as we drove toward the Lyceum Theatre. "He and Papa were in command of the prison camp in India. They were therefore together a great deal. By the way, a curious paper was found in Papa's desk. No one could understand it. I don't suppose it is of the slightest importance. But I thought you might care to see it, so I brought it with me. It is here."

Holmes unfolded the paper carefully and smoothed it upon his knee. He then examined it with his magnifying glass.

"It is paper made in India," he remarked. "It has at sometime been pinned to a board. The diagram upon it appears to be part of a large building with numerous halls, corridors, and passages. At one point is a small cross in red ink. Above it is '3.37 from left' in faded pencil-writing. In the left-hand corner is a curious figure that looks like four crosses in a line with their arms touching. Beside it is written, 'The sign of the four—Jonathan Small, Mahomet Singh, Abdullah Khan, Dost Akbar.' No, I confess that I do not see how it bears on the matter. Yet, it is clearly a document of importance. It has been kept carefully in a wallet, for one side is as clean as the other."

"It was in his wallet that we found it."

"Preserve it carefully, Miss Morstan. It may prove of use to us. I begin to suspect that this matter is deeper than I first thought. I must reconsider my ideas." He leaned back in the cab. I could see by his drawn brow and his blank stare that he was thinking intently. Miss Morstan and I chatted quietly about our adventure and its possible outcome. But Holmes remained quiet until we had reached our destination.

It was a September evening and not yet seven, but the day had been a dreary one. A dense, drizzly fog lay low over the great city. Dark clouds drooped sadly over the muddy streets. The street lamps were but misty splotches of light upon the slimy pavement. There was something about the night and our strange errand that made me nervous and depressed. I could see from Miss Morstan's manner that she was suffering from the same feeling. Holmes alone remained indifferent to the mood. He held his open notebook upon his knee and from time to time jotted down figures and notes.

At the Lyceum Theatre the crowds were beginning to form at the entrances. We went to the third pillar on the left. A small, dark man came up to us immediately.

"Did you come with Miss Morstan?" he asked Holmes.

"I am Miss Morstan, and these two gentlemen are my friends," she replied.

"You will excuse me, miss," he said, "but I must ask you to give your word that neither of your friends is a police officer."

"I give you my word on that," she answered.

He gave a shrill whistle. A cab pulled up. The man mounted the box and we took our places inside. The driver whipped up his horse. We plunged away at a furious pace through the foggy streets.

The situation was a curious one. We were driving to an unknown place, on an unknown errand. Our journey was either a complete hoax—which seemed unlikely—or else important issues hung on it. Miss Morstan was as cool and collected as ever. I tried to cheer and amuse her with tales of my adventures in Afghanistan. To tell the truth, I was myself so excited at our situation that my stories were slightly confused. To this day she remembers one moving story as to how a musket looked into my tent at the dead of night and how I fired a double-barreled tiger cub at it. At first I had some idea of the direction we were driving, but soon our pace and the fog made me lose my bearings. However, Sherlock Holmes knew exactly where we were going. He muttered the name of each road we passed.

"Rochester Row," said he. "Now Vincent Square. Now we come out on the Vauxhall Bridge Road. We are making for the Surrey side. Yes, I thought so. Now we are on the bridge. You can catch glimpses of the river."

We did get a fleeting view of the river. But the cab dashed on.

"Wordsworth Road," said my companion. "Priory Road. Lark Hall Lane. Stockwell Place. Robert Street. Cold Harbor Lane. Our quest does not appear to take us to very fashionable regions."

We had, indeed, reached a questionable and forbidding neighborhood. At last the cab drew up at a dull brick house. None of the other houses in the lane were lived in. The one we stopped at was as dark as its neighbors, except for a single glimmer in the kitchen window. However, on our knocking, an Indian servant opened the door. He was dressed in a yellow turban, white loose-fitting clothes and a yellow sash.

"My master awaits you," said he. As he spoke there came a high piping voice from some inner room. "Show them in to me," it cried. "Show them straight in to me."

Chapter 4
The Story of the
Bald-headed Man

We followed the Indian down a dark and dingy passage. At last he came to a door on the right. This he threw open. A blaze of yellow light streamed out upon us. In the center of the glare stood a small man. His head was bald except for a circle of red hair all around the edge. He seemed to be in constant motion, now smiling, now frowning. His lip trembled and his hands shook. His face looked young. Despite his baldness, he was no more than thirty years of age.

"Your servant, Miss Morstan," he kept repeating in a thin, high voice. "Your servant, gentlemen. Please step into my little castle. A small place, miss, but furnished to my liking."

We were all astonished at the appearance of the room. It was decorated in the most rich and lavish fashion. Curtains and tapestries draped the walls. The carpet was so soft and thick that the foot sank pleasantly into it. Two great tiger skins were thrown across it and added to the sense of eastern luxury. A large brass hookah, or water pipe, stood in a corner. A lamp in the shape of a silver dove hung from an almost invisible golden wire. As it burned it filled the air with incense.

"Mr. Thaddeus Sholto," said the little man. "That is

my name. You are Miss Morstan, of course. And these gentlemen—"

"This is Mr. Sherlock Holmes, and this is Dr. Watson."

"A doctor, eh," cried he, much excited. "Have you your stethoscope? I have been much worried about my heart—would you mind listening to it? I should value your opinion."

I listened to his heart, but could find nothing wrong. "It appears to be normal," I said. "You have no cause for uneasiness."

"You will excuse my anxiety, Miss Morstan," he remarked. "I have long been worried about my heart. Had your father put less strain upon his, he might be alive now."

I could have struck the man across the face for his thoughtless remark. Miss Morstan sat down. Her face grew white to the lips. "I knew in my heart that he was dead," said she.

"I can give you all the information," said he. "And what is more, I can give you justice—and I will, too—whatever my brother, Bartholomew, may say! I am so glad to have your friends here. Both as an escort to you and as witnesses to what I am about to do and say. The four of us can stand strong against Brother Bartholomew. But let us have no outsiders—no police or officials. We can settle everything among ourselves. Nothing would annoy Brother Bartholomew more than publicity." He sat down upon a low settee and blinked at us with his weak, watery blue eyes.

"For my part," said Holmes, "whatever you may choose to say will go no further."

I nodded to show my agreement.

"That is well! That is well!" said he. "May I offer you a glass of wine? Shall I open a flask? No? Well, I trust that you have no objection to tobacco smoke. I am a little nervous and find my hookah a comfort." He filled his large water pipe with tobacco and began to smoke through its hose. We all three sat in a semicircle while he puffed uneasily in the center.

"I would have given you my address," said Thaddeus Sholto, "but I feared you would bring unpleasant people with you. I therefore made the appointment at the theatre. That way my man, William, could see you first. You will excuse me taking such precautions, but I do not like offensive people. As you can see I live in an atmosphere of elegance . . ."

"You will excuse me, Mr. Sholto," said Miss Morstan. "But I am here to learn something which you desire to tell me. It is late and I should like the interview to be as short as possible."

"At the very best it must take some time," he answered. "We shall certainly have to go to Norwood and see Brother Bartholomew. We shall all go and try to convince him what I am doing is right. He is very upset with me right now about this matter. I had some angry words with him last night. You cannot imagine what a terrible fellow he is when he is angry."

"Since it is late, perhaps we should leave at once," I said.

He laughed until his ears were quite red. "That would hardly do," he cried. "No, I must tell you the entire story first. There are several points of the story which I myself do not know. But I will tell you all the facts I know."

"My father was Major John Sholto, once of the Indian army. He retired some eleven years ago. He returned to England and lived at Pondicherry Lodge in Upper Norwood. He had done well in India and brought back a considerable sum of money, a large collection of art objects, and a staff of native servants. My twin brother Bartholomew and I were his only children.

"I very well remember the sensation which was caused by the disappearance of Captain Morstan. We read the details in the papers. We knew that he was a friend of our father and discussed the case in his presence. He used to join in our speculations about what could have happened. Never did we suspect that he alone knew the fate of Arthur Morstan.

"We did know that some danger hung over our father. He was very fearful of going out alone. He had two prizefighters as porters at the lodge. William, who drove you tonight, was one of them. He was once lightweight champion of England. Our father would never tell us what he feared. But he disliked men with wooden legs. Once he actually fired his revolver at a wooden-legged man. The man turned out to be a harmless tradesman. We had to pay a large sum to hush the matter up. My brother and I used to think this was just a whim of my father's. But events have since led us to change our opinion.

"Early in 1882 my father received a letter from India. It was a great shock to him. He nearly fainted at the breakfast table on reading it. From that day on he was a sick man. He never recovered. We never discovered what was in the letter. I could see as he held it that it was short and written in a scrawling hand. For years he had suffered from an enlarged spleen. He became rapidly worse. In April we were told that he was beyond hope and that he wished to speak with us one last time.

"When we entered his room he was propped up with pillows and breathing heavily. He told us to lock the door and come up on either side of the bed. Then he grasped our hands. He told us a remarkable statement. As he spoke his voice was broken as much by emotion as by pain. I shall try and give you it in his very own words.

" 'Only one thing weighs upon my mind,' he said. 'It is my treatment of poor Morstan's orphan. Greed has been my sin throughout my life. It stopped me from parting with the treasure, which is half hers. And yet I have made no use of it myself. But I could not bear to share it with another. See that necklace studded with pearls beside the quinine bottle . . . ? Even that I could not bear to part with, although I got it out to send to her. You, my sons, will give her a fair share of the Agra treasure. But send her nothing, not even the necklace, until I am gone.

" 'I will tell you how Morstan died,' he continued. 'He had suffered for years from a weak heart, but he hid it from everyone. I alone knew it. When we were in India we came into possession of a considerable treasure. I brought it over to England. Morstan came straight here for his share on the night he arrived. He walked over from the station. He was let in by my faithful servant, Lal Chowdar, who is now dead. Morstan and I disagreed on how the treasure should be divided. We began to argue. Morstan sprang out of his chair in anger. Suddenly he pressed his hand to his side. His face turned pale and he fell back. His head cut against the corner of the treasure chest in the fall. I stooped over him. To my horror, he was dead.

" 'For a long time I sat wondering what I should do. My first thought was to call for help. But then I saw that I might be accused of murder. The fact that he died in a quarrel and had a gash in his head did not look good. And suppose there was an official inquiry. Certain facts would come out about the treasure—facts I wanted to keep secret. He had told me that no soul on earth knew where he had gone. There seemed no reason why any soul should ever know.

" 'I was pondering over what to do, when I looked up. There stood my servant, Lal Chowdar. He came in and bolted the door behind him. "Do not fear, master," he said. "No one need know that you have killed him. Let us hide him away." "I did not kill him," said I. Lal Chowdar shook his head and smiled. "I heard it all, master. I heard you quarrel, and I heard the blow. But my lips are sealed. All are asleep in the house. Let us hide him together." That was enough to decide me. If my own servant could not believe my innocence, how could I hope to make a jury believe me? Lal Chowdar and I disposed of the body that night. Within a few days the newspapers were full of the mysterious disappearance of Captain Morstan. You can see that I could not be blamed for what I did. My fault lay in clinging to the treasure since his death. I wish to make it up to his orphan. Put your ears down to my mouth. The treasure is hidden in—' At this instant a horrible change came over him. His eyes stared wildly, his jaw dropped and he yelled in a terrible voice, 'Keep him out! For Christ's sake keep him out!' His gaze was fixed on the window. We both turned round. A face was looking in at us out of the darkness. It was a bearded, hairy face with cruel eyes. My brother and I rushed toward the window. But the man was gone. We returned to my father. His head was dropped and his pulse had ceased to beat.

"We searched the garden that night. We found no sign of the intruder. But under the window there was a single footmark. In the morning the window of my father's bedroom was open. His cupboards and boxes had been rifled. On his chest was fixed a torn piece of paper. The words 'The sign of the four' were scrawled across it. We never knew what it meant. Nor did we ever learn who our visitor was. Everything was turned upside down, but nothing seemed stolen. Of course, we figured this was the man our father had feared. But the matter is still a complete mystery to us."

The little man stopped to relight his pipe. We all sat quietly listening to his extraordinary story. Miss Morstan had turned deadly white on hearing the account of her father's death. For a moment I had feared that she was going to faint. I had quietly poured her a glass of water from a side table. This had seemed to help. Sherlock Holmes leaned back in his chair with his eyes closed. Just that day he had complained that he needed brainwork. Here was a problem to tax his brain. Mr. Thaddeus Sholto looked from one to the other of us. He was clearly proud of the effect his story had upon us.

"My brother and I," he continued, "were much

excited about the treasure. For weeks and for months we dug up the garden. But we did not discover its whereabouts. It was maddening to think its hiding place was on his lips when he died. We knew that the treasure must be incredible as the necklace was magnificent. Bartholomew and I argued over the necklace. The pearls were clearly of great value. He did not want to part with them. And he thought that if we parted with the necklace, it could give rise to gossip. At last I persuaded him to let me find Miss Morstan. I would send her one pearl a year. In this way, she would never feel without security."

"It was a kindly thought," said our companion. "It was extremely good of you."

The little man waved his hand. "We were your trustees. That was the view which I took. My brother could not quite see it in that light. We had plenty of money ourselves. I desired no more. Our difference of opinion on this went so far that I moved out of Pondicherry Lodge. I took two servants with me. Yesterday my brother summoned me. He had discovered the treasure. I instantly contacted Miss Morstan. I want us now to drive to Norwood and demand our share. I explained my views to Brother Bartholomew last night. We shall be expected, if not welcome."

We all sat silent for some time. Holmes was the first to speak.

"You have done well, sir, from first to last," said he. "It is late and we had best depart without delay."

Sholto slowly coiled up his pipe. Then he took out a fur coat. He buttoned this up tightly, in spite of the warm weather outside. Then he put on a rabbit-skin cap with hanging earflaps. No part of him could be seen but his face. "My health is somewhat fragile," he remarked.

Our cab was waiting for us outside. The driver started off at a rapid pace. Thaddeus Sholto talked constantly in a shrill voice.

"Bartholomew is a clever fellow," said he. "How do you think he found the treasure? He had come to the conclusion that it was indoors. So he worked out the cubic space of the house. Then he made measurements everywhere. He found that the height of the building was seventy-four feet. He added the heights of all the rooms and the space in between them. But he could not bring the total to more than seventy feet. Four feet were missing. These could only be at the top of the building under the roof. He knocked a hole in the ceiling of his laboratory which was the highest room. Sure enough, there was a little garrett above it. It had been sealed up and was known to no one. In the center stood the treasure chest. He lowered it through the hole and there it lies. He figures the value of the jewels is over half a million."

We all stared at one another open-eyed. If Miss Morstan received half the treasure, she would change from a needy governess to one of the richest heiresses in England. I knew I should be happy at the thought of her good fortune. But my heart turned heavy as lead. Such a wealthy woman could clearly not be interested in a lowly army doctor such as I.

Chapter 5
The Tragedy of
Pondicherry Lodge

It was nearly eleven o'clock when we reached the final stage of our night's adventure. Thaddeus Sholto took down one of the side-lamps from the carriage.

"This is Pondicherry Lodge," he said to Miss Morstan. The house stood in its own grounds. A very high stone wall surrounded it. The only entrance was a narrow iron-framed gate. He knocked on this entrance with a peculiar rat-tat.

"Who is it?" cried a gruff voice from within.

"It is I, McMurdo. You surely know my knock by this time."

There was a grumbling sound and a clanking of keys. The gate swung heavily back. A short, deep-chested man stood in the opening.

"That you, Mr. Thaddeus? But who are the others? I had no orders about them from the master."

"No, McMurdo? You surprise me! I told my brother last night that I should bring some friends."

"He hain't been out of his room today, Mr. Thaddeus. And I have no orders. You know very well that I must stick to rules. I can let you in, but your friends must stop where they are."

This was an unexpected obstacle. Thaddeus Sholto looked about him in a helpless, upset manner. "This is really bad of you, McMurdo!" he said. "If I say they are friends, that should be enough for you. And there is the young lady. She can't wait on the public road at this hour."

"Very sorry, Mr. Thaddeus," said the man. "They may be your friends, but not friends of the master. He pays me well to do my duty. And my duty I'll do. I don't know none of your friends."

"Oh, yes, you do, McMurdo," cried Sherlock Holmes. "I don't think you can forget me. Don't you remember the amateur boxer who fought three rounds with you at Alison's rooms four years back?"

"Not Mr. Sherlock Holmes!" roared the prizefighter. "God's truth! How could I have mistook you? Why did you stand there so quiet? You should have stepped up and given me that cross-hit of yours under the jaw. I'd have known you right away! You're one that has wasted your gifts, you have. You might have been a great fighter."

"You see, Watson. If all else fails I can always take up fighting!" said Holmes, laughing. "Our friend won't keep us out in the cold now, I am sure."

"In you come, sir, in you come—you and your friends," he answered. "Very sorry, Mr. Thaddeus, but orders are very strict. Had to be certain of your friends before I let them in."

Inside the wall, a gravel path wound through the grounds to the house. The house was in darkness, except where a moonbeam struck one corner and glimmered in a high window. It was a huge house and loomed above us gloomily. Even Thaddeus seemed ill at ease. The lantern quivered and rattled in his hand.

"I cannot understand it," he said. "There must be some mistake. I distinctly told Bartholomew that we were coming. Yet there is no light in his window. I do not know what to make of it."

"Does he always guard the premises in this way?" asked Holmes.

"Yes, he has followed my father's custom. He was the favorite son, you know. I sometimes think that my father may have told him more than he told me. That is Bartholomew's window up there where the moonshine strikes. It is quite bright, but there is no light from within, I think."

"None," said Holmes. "But I see the glint of a light in that little window beside the door."

"Ah, that is the housekeeper's room, that is where old Mrs. Bernstone sits. She can tell us all about it. Please wait here a moment or two. But hush! What is that?"

He held up a lantern. His hand shook, until the circles of light flickered and wavered about us. Miss Morstan seized my wrist. We all stood with thumping hearts, straining our ears. From the great black house there came the shrill, whimpering of a frightened woman.

"It is Mrs. Bernstone," said Sholto. "She is the only woman in the house. Wait here. I shall be back in a moment." He hurried for the door and knocked in his peculiar way. We could see a tall old woman let him in. She swayed with pleasure at the very sight of him.

"Oh, Mr. Thaddeus, sir, I am so glad you have come!

I am so glad you have come, Mr. Thaddeus, sir!" Then the door was closed and we could hear no more.

Our guide had left us the lantern. Holmes swung it slowly and peered at the house and the grounds. Giant rubbish heaps were scattered all about. Miss Morstan and I stood together, her hand still in mine. We had never seen each other before that day and yet in that hour of trouble our hands sought each other. I have marveled at it since, but at that time it seemed the most natural thing in the world.

"What a strange place!" she said, looking around.

"It looks as though all the moles in England had been let loose in it."

"These are the traces of the treasure-seekers," said Sherlock Holmes. "You must remember that for six years they have been looking for it. No wonder the grounds look like a gravel pit."

At that moment the door of the house burst open. Thaddeus Sholto came running out. Terror was in his eyes.

"There is something wrong with Bartholomew!" he cried. "I am frightened! My nerves cannot stand it." He was half blubbering with fear.

"Come into the house," said Holmes, in a crisp, firm way.

"Yes, do!" pleaded Thaddeus Sholto. "I really can't give any directions myself."

We all followed him into the housekeeper's room. The old woman was pacing up and down. The sight of Miss Morstan seemed to soothe her.

"God bless your sweet calm face!" she cried. "It does me good to see you."

Miss Morstan patted the woman's thin work-worn hand and murmured some words of comfort.

"Master has locked himself in and will not answer me," she explained. "All day I have waited to hear from him. An hour ago I feared something was wrong. So I went up and peeped through the keyhole. You must go up, Mr. Thaddeus. You must go up and look for yourself. I have seen Mr. Bartholomew be happy and sad, but I have never seen the look that he had on his face."

We left Miss Morstan with the old woman. Sherlock Holmes took the lamp and led the way, for Thaddeus Sholto's teeth were chattering in his head. As we walked up the stairs, Holmes examined marks with his magnifying glass. To me they looked like nothing more than shapeless smudges of dust upon the floormatting. He walked slowly from step to step, looking carefully left and right.

The third flight of stairs ended in a landing. Three doors were on the left. The third was Mr. Bartholomew's. Holmes knocked but received no answer. Then he tried to turn the handle. It was locked from within by a broad and powerful bolt. The keyhole, however, was clear. Holmes bent down and looked through it.

"There is something devilish in this, Watson," said Holmes. He seemed more upset than I had ever seen him. "What do you make of it?"

I stooped to the hole and recoiled in horror. Moonlight was streaming into the room. Looking straight at me was a face—the very face of our companion, Thaddeus. There was the same shining head, the same fringe of red hair, the same paleness. But the features were set in a horrible smile. It was so unnatural that it made my skin crawl. The face was so like Thaddeus' that I turned around to make sure he was still beside us. Then I recalled that they were twins.

"This is terrible!" I said to Holmes. "What is to be done?"

"The door must come down," he answered. He banged his body against it. It creaked and groaned but did not open. Together we flung ourselves upon it once more. This time it gave way with a sudden snap. We found ourselves in Bartholomew Sholto's chemical laboratory.

In the center of the room was a table. It was littered with bunsen burners and glass bottles. In the corner stood a number of barrels of creosote—an oily liquid made from wood tar. One had been broken and the dark liquid had trickled out from it. The air was heavy with the tarlike odor. A stepladder stood to one side of the room. Plaster was strewn around it. Above, there was an opening in the ceiling. It was just large enough for a man to pass through. At the base of the ladder was a long coil of rope.

In a wooden armchair was the master of the house. He was all in a heap with his head sunk upon his left shoulder. That ghastly smile was upon his face. He was stiff and cold. He had clearly been dead for some hours. His features and his limbs were twisted in the most fantastic manner. On the table beside him lay a brown stick. A piece of stone had been attached to one end with coarse twine. Beside it was a torn sheet of paper. Some words were scrawled upon it. Holmes glanced at it. Then he handed it to me.

In the light of the lantern I read, "The sign of the four." A thrill of terror went through me.

"In God's name, what does it all mean?" I asked.

"It means murder," said Sherlock Holmes. He stepped over the dead man. "Ah, I expected it. Look here!" He pointed to what looked like a long, dark thorn stuck in the skin just above the ear.

"It looks like a thorn," said I.

"It is a wooden thorn. You may pick it up. But be careful, for it is poisoned."

I took it up between my finger and my thumb. It came away from the skin readily. There was hardly any mark left in the skin. One tiny speck of blood showed where the puncture had been.

"This is a complete mystery to me," said I. "It grows darker instead of clearer."

"On the contrary," said Sherlock Holmes. "It clears every instant. I only require a few missing links to have an entirely connected case."

We had almost forgotten poor Mr. Thaddeus Sholto. He was still standing in the doorway. He was the very picture of terror. He was wringing his hands and moaning to himself. Suddenly he broke out into a sharp cry.

"The treasure is gone!" he said. "They have robbed him of the treasure! There is the hole through which we lowered it. I helped him to do it! I was the last person who saw him! I left him here last night. I heard him lock the door as I came down the stairs!"

"What time was that?"

"It was ten o'clock. And now he is dead and the police will be called in. I shall be suspected of having a hand in it. Oh yes, I am sure I shall. Don't you think so, gentlemen? Surely you don't think that it was I? Would I have brought you here? Oh dear! Oh dear! I know that I shall go mad." He jerked his arms and stamped his feet hysterically.

"You have no reason to fear, Mr. Sholto," said Holmes. He put his hand upon his shoulder. "Take my advice, and drive down to the station. Report the matter to the police. Offer to assist them in every way. We shall wait here until you return."

The little man obeyed without saying another word. We heard him stumbling down the stairs in the dark.

Chapter 6
Sherlock Holmes Gives a Demonstration

"Now, Watson," said Holmes. "We have half an hour to ourselves. Let us make use of it. My case is almost complete. Simple as the case may seem now, there may be something deeper to it."

"Simple!" I exclaimed.

"Surely," said he. "Sit in the corner there. Your footprints will just complicate things. Now to work! In the first place, how did these folk come and how did they go? The door had not been opened since last night. By the window?" He carried the lamp across to it. "Let me see. There are no hinges at the side. It is fastened shut. Let us open it. No waterpipe near. Roof quite out of reach. Yet a man has entered by it. It rained a little last night. Here is the print of a foot upon the sill. And here is a circular muddy mark, and here again upon the floor. And here upon the table. See here, Watson."

I looked at the round muddy prints. "This is not a footmark," said I.

"It is something much more valuable to us. It is the impression of a wooden stump. You see here on the sill is the boot mark. It is a heavy boot with a broad metal heel. Beside it is the mark of a wooden leg."

"The wooden-legged man!" I exclaimed.

"Quite so. But there has been someone else here. Someone who was very valuable to him. Could you scale that wall, Doctor?"

I looked out the open window. The moon still shone brightly on this side of the house. We were a good sixty feet from the ground. I could see nothing that could be used as a foothold. There was not as much as a crevice in the brickwork.

"It is absolutely impossible," I answered.

"Without aid it is so. But suppose you had a friend up here. He could lower you this stout rope. Suppose he attached one end to this great hook in the wall. Then, I think, you could climb up the wall, wooden leg and all. You would leave in the same fashion. Your friend would draw up the rope, untie it from the hook, and shut the window. Then he would get away the same way he came. I see with my magnifying glass blood marks at the end of the rope. He must have slipped down so quickly that he took off the skin of his hand."

"This is all very well," said I. "But the thing becomes even more difficult to understand. How about this mysterious friend? How did he come into the room?"

"Yes, this friend," repeated Holmes. "There are features of interest about this friend. He lifts this case above the ordinary. I fancy that he is a first in the history of crime."

"How came he then?" I repeated. "The door is locked. The window is impossible to reach. Was it through the chimney?"

"The grate is much too small," Holmes answered. "I had already considered that."

"How then?" I persisted.

"When you eliminate the impossible, whatever remains must be the truth. We know he did not come through the door, the window, or the chimney. We also know that he could not have been hidden in the room, as there is no cover. Whence, then, did he come?"

"He came through the hole in the roof!" I cried.

"Of course he did. He must have done so. Please hold up the lamp for me. We shall now examine the room above—the secret room where the treasure was found."

He mounted the steps. He seized a hold of the beam and swung himself into the small chamber. He lay on his face and reached down for the lamp. Then I followed him up.

The chamber was about ten feet one way and six the other. The floor was made of thin strips of wood and plaster. This meant that one had to walk from beam to beam. There was no furniture of any sort and years of dust lay on the floor.

"Here you are, you see," said Sherlock Holmes. He put his hand against the sloping wall of the true roof. "Here is a trapdoor which leads out onto the roof. I can press it back. This is the way in which Number One entered. Let us see if we can find some other traces of him."

He held the lamp to the floor. A startled look came over his face. I followed his gaze. What I saw made me turn cold. The floor was covered with the dark prints of a bare foot. It was a clear, perfectly formed foot. But it was half the size of those of an ordinary man.

"Holmes," I said, in a whisper, "a child has done this horrid thing."

"I was staggered for a moment," he said. "But the thing is quite natural. My memory failed me. There is nothing more to learn here. Let us go down."

We clambered down the steps once again.

"What is your theory as to those footprints?" I asked eagerly.

"My dear Watson. Try to deduce it yourself. You know my methods. Apply them. It will be interesting for us to compare our theories."

"I cannot think of any theory to cover the facts," I answered.

"It will be clear enough to you soon," said Sherlock Holmes. "I think there is nothing more of importance here, but I will look." He whipped out his magnifying glass and a tape measure. Then he hurried about the room on his knees. He measured, compared, examined with his long, thin nose only inches from the planks. As he hunted he kept muttering to himself. At last he broke out into a loud crow of delight.

"We are certainly in luck," said he. "We ought to have little trouble now. Number One has stepped into the creosote. You can see the outline of his small foot here—right at the edge of this evil-smelling mess."

"So what?"

"Why, we've got him, that's all," said he. "I know a dog that would follow this scent to the world's end. But hallo, here comes the law."

Heavy steps and loud voices could be heard from downstairs.

"Before they come," said Holmes, "just put your hand here on this poor fellow's arm, and here on his leg. What do you feel?"

"The muscles are as hard as a board," I answered.

"Quite so. They are much harder than is usual. Now look at the expression on his face. What does this suggest to you."

"Death by strong poison," said I.

"Exactly. That is what I thought when I saw the drawn muscles of his face. Then I discovered a thorn in his scalp. It had been driven or shot with great force. When Sholto was sitting erect, that part of the scalp would have been turned upward toward the hole in the ceiling. Now examine this thorn."

I took it up and held it to the light. It was long, sharp and black. Some gummy substance had dried at its tip. The blunt end had been trimmed and rounded off with a knife.

"Is that an English thorn?" Holmes asked.

"No, it is certainly not."

"With all this information you should certainly be able to draw some conclusions. But here come the police."

A very stout, broad man entered the room. He was followed by an inspector in uniform. Behind them came Thaddeus Sholto, still jerking and twitching.

"Here's a business!" cried the fat man in a husky voice. "Here's a pretty business! But who are these two? Why, the house seems to be as full as a rabbit-warren!"

"I think you must recollect me, Mr. Athelney Jones," said Sherlock Holmes, quietly.

"Why, of course I do!" he wheezed. "It's Mr. Sherlock Holmes. Remember you! I'll never forget how you lectured us on the Bishopsgate jewel case. All about observation and deduction. It's true you set us on the right track. But you have to admit now that it was more luck than good guidance."

"It was a piece of very simple reasoning."

"Oh, come, now, come!" said Jones. "Never be ashamed to admit the truth. But what's all this? Bad business. How lucky that I happened to be in Norwood on another case! I was at the station when the message arrived. What d'you think the man died of?"

"Oh, this is hardly a case for me to lecture you on," said Holmes.

"No, no. Still, we can't deny that you hit the nail on the head sometimes. Dear me! Door locked, I understand. Jewels worth half a million missing. How was the window?"

"Fastened, but there were footprints on the sill," replied Holmes.

"Well, well, if it was fastened then the prints could have nothing to do with the matter. That's common sense. Man might have died in a fit, but then the jewels are missing. Ha! I have a theory. These flashes come to me sometimes. Just step outside, sergeant, and you, Mr. Sholto. Holmes, your friend can remain. What do you think of this, Holmes? Sholto admitted that he was with his brother last night. The brother died in a fit. Then Sholto walked off with the treasure. How's that?"

"And then the dead man got up and locked the door from the inside."

"Hum. There's a flaw there. Let us apply common sense to the matter. This Thaddeus Sholto *was* with his brother; there was a quarrel; so much we know. The brother is dead and the jewels are gone. So much also we know. No one saw the brother from the time Thaddeus left him. His bed had not been slept in. Thaddeus clearly is in a disturbed state of mind. You see that I am weaving a web around Thaddeus. The net begins to close upon him."

"You do not have all the facts." said Holmes. "This splinter of wood, which I believe is poisoned, was in the man's scalp. You can still see the mark. This note was on the table. Beside it lay this rather curious stone-headed instrument. How does all that fit into your theory?"

"Confirms it in every respect," said the fat detective. "House is full of Indian curiosities. Thaddeus brought the thorn and weapon up. If the thorn is indeed poisoned, well, Thaddeus could have put poison on it as well as any other. The note is some hocus-pocus—to throw us off the scent. The only question is, how did he depart? Ah, of course, here is a hole in the roof." Despite his size, he sprang up the ladder and squeezed into the chamber. Immediately afterward we heard him crow that he had found the trapdoor.

"He can find something," remarked Holmes. "Once in a while he can figure something out."

"You see!" said Athelney Jones, coming down the steps. "My view of the case is confirmed. There is a trapdoor to the roof. It is partly open."

"It was I who opened it," said Holmes.

"Oh, indeed! You did notice it, then?" He seemed disappointed at this. "Well, anyway, it shows how our gentleman got away. Sergeant!"

"Yes, sir," from the passage.

"Ask Mr. Sholto to step this way. Mr. Sholto, it is my duty to inform you that anything which you say will be used against you. I arrest you in the Queen's name as being concerned in the death of your brother."

"There, now! Didn't I tell you!" cried the poor little man. He threw up his hands and looked from one to the other of us.

"Don't trouble yourself about it, Mr. Sholto," said Holmes. "I think I can clear you of the charge."

"Don't promise too much, Mr. Holmes—don't promise too much," snapped the detective. "You may find it a harder matter than you think."

"I will clear him, Mr. Jones. And I will tell you the name of one of the two people who were in this room last night. His name, I believe, is Jonathan Small. He is a small, active man and his right leg is gone. He wears a wooden stump and it is worn away on the inner side. His left boot is square-toed with an iron band round the heel. He is middle-aged, much sunburned and has been a convict. These are a few deductions to help you. Oh, there is a good deal of skin missing from the palm of his hand. The other man—"

"The other man—?" asked Athelney Jones.

"Is a rather curious person," said Sherlock Holmes. With that he turned on his heel. "I hope to introduce you to the pair of them soon. A word with you, Watson."

He led me out to the head of the stair. "This murder has caused us to lose sight of our reason for being here."

"I have just been thinking the same thing," I answered. "It is not right that Miss Morstan should remain in the house."

"No. You must escort her home. She lives with Mrs. Cecil Forrester, in Lower Camberwell. It is not far. I will wait for you here. Or perhaps you are too tired."

"By no means. I don't think I could rest until I know more of this fantastic business."

"Your presence will be of great service to me," he answered. "We shall work the case out alone. We will leave this fellow Jones to guess what he will. Drop Miss Morstan off and then go to 3 Pinchin Lane. It is the third house on the right-hand side and belongs to a bird-stuffer. Sherman is the name. You will see a stuffed weasel holding a young stuffed rabbit in the window. Wake old Sherman up and tell him that I need Toby at once. You will bring Toby back in the cab with you."

"A dog, I suppose?"

"Yes, a queer mongrel, with a most amazing power of scent. I would rather have Toby's help than that of the whole detective force of London."

"I shall bring him, then," said I. "It is one now. I ought to be back before three."

"And I," said Holmes, "shall see what I can learn from Mrs. Bernstone and from the Indian servant. Thaddeus tells me he sleeps next to that hidden chamber. Then I shall listen to the ravings of that would-be detective, Mr. Athelney Jones."

Chapter 7
The Episode of the Barrel

The police had brought a cab with them. I took Miss Morstan home in it. I found her bearing the trouble with a calm face. She was bright and cheerful by the side of the frightened housekeeper. Once in the cab, however, she turned faint and then burst into tears. Later she told me that I was very cold and distant in that cab. She did not know then how much, in that one day, I had come to care for her. But in my mind the Agra treasure stood between us. If Holmes solved the case, she would be rich. She might think me a fortune hunter. So I kept my distance.

It was nearly two o'clock when we reached Mrs. Cecil Forrester's. The strange message that Miss Morstan had received had interested Mrs. Forrester. She had stayed up to find out what it was all about. She urged me to come in and explain the matter. But I told Mrs. Forrester and Miss Morstan of my important errand and promised to inform them of any new developments.

The more I thought about what had happened, the wilder and darker it grew. As I rattled through the silent, gaslit streets, I reviewed the whole extraordinary sequence of events. The original mystery was pretty clear now: the death of Captain Morstan, the sending of the pearl, the advertisement, the letter. We had learned a great deal about these things. They had led us, however, to a deeper and far more tragic mystery: the Indian treasure, the curious diagram found among Morstan's baggage, the strange scene at Major Sholto's death, the rediscovery of the treasure, the murder of its discoverer, the strange manner of the death, the footprints, the odd

weapons, the words on the note—the same as those on Captain Morstan's diagram. How did it all fit together?

Pinchin Lane was a row of shabby two-storied brick houses. I had to knock three times at number 3 before someone answered. At last I saw the glint of a candle. A face looked out of the window.

"Go away," said the face. "If you make any more noise, I'll open the kennels and let out forty-three dogs upon you."

"I only want one," said I.

"Go away!" yelled the voice.

"But I want a dog," I cried.

"I won't be argued with!" shouted Mr. Sherman.

"Mr. Sherlock Holmes—" I began. The words had the most magical effect. Within a minute the door was unlocked. Mr. Sherman was a lean old man with stooping shoulders and blue-tinted glasses.

"A friend of Mr. Sherlock Holmes is always welcome," said he. "Step in, sir. Keep clear of the badger, he bites. What was it that Mr. Sherlock Holmes wanted, sir?"

"He wanted a dog of yours," I said.

"Ah! That would be Toby."

"Yes. Toby was the name."

"Toby lives on the left here." He moved slowly forward with his candle. "Mind the animals." In the dim light I could see eyes peeping down at us from every corner. Even the beams above our heads were lined with birds. I could hear them shifting their weight from one leg to another.

Toby turned out to be an ugly, long-haired creature. The old man handed me a sugar cube which I gave to him. We quickly became friends. He followed me into the cab with no problem. It had struck three by the time I reached Pondicherry Lodge. Two policemen now guarded the narrow gate.

Holmes was standing on the doorstep. His hands were in his pockets and he was smoking a pipe.

"Ah, you have him there!" said he. "Good dog. Athelney Jones has gone. He has arrested not only our friend Thaddeus, but the gatekeeper, the housekeeper and the Indian servant. We have the place to ourselves, except for a sergeant upstairs. Leave the dog here and come up."

We tied Toby to the hall table and went up the stairs. The room was as we had left it, except a sheet was now draped over the victim. A weary-looking police sergeant lounged in the corner.

"Tie this bit of rope around my waist," said Holmes. "Thank you. Now I must kick off my boots and stockings—just carry them outside when you go. I am going to do a little climbing. And dip my handkerchief in the creosote there. That will do. Now come into the chamber with me a moment."

We clambered up through the hole. Holmes turned his light once more on the footprints in the dust.

"Take a good look at these footprints," said he. "Do you notice anything special about them?"

"They belong to a child or a small woman," I answered.

"Besides their size. Is there anything else?"

"No. They look just like any other footprints."

"Not at all. Look here! This is the print of the right

foot in the dust. Now I make one with my bare foot beside it. What is the chief difference?"

"Your toes are cramped together. The other print has each toe distinctly divided."

"Quite so. That is the point. Bear that in mind. Now would you step over to the trapdoor and smell the edge of the woodwork."

I did as he directed. I was instantly aware of a strong tarry smell.

"That is where he put his foot in getting out. If you can smell him, I should think that Toby will have no difficulty. Now run downstairs and let loose the dog outside."

By the time Toby and I were outside, Sherlock Holmes was on the roof. He carried the lantern in his hand. I could see him crawling slowly along the ridge. For a while I lost sight of him behind a stack of chimneys. Then he reappeared on the opposite side of the house. I made my way around to him. I found him seated on one of the corner eaves.

"That you, Watson?" he cried.

"Yes."

"This is the place. What is that black thing down there?"

"A water barrel," I said.

"Top on it?"

"Yes."

"No sign of a ladder?" he asked.

"No."

"The waterpipe seems pretty firm. Well, here goes."

There was a scuffling of feet and the lantern began

to come down the side of the wall. Then with a light spring Holmes came onto the barrel, and from there to the earth.

"It was easy to follow him," said Holmes as he put on his stockings and boots. "Tiles were loosened all along the way. In his hurry he dropped this."

The object he held was a small pocket or pouch. It was woven out of colored grasses and a few beads were strung to it. Its shape and size was like a cigarette case. Inside were half a dozen thorns of dark wood. Each was sharp at one end and rounded at the other—just like that which had struck Bartholomew Sholto.

"They are hellish things," said he. "Look out that you don't prick yourself. I'm delighted to have them. They are most likely all he has. Now there is less fear that we will find one in our skin before long. Are you up for a six-mile hike, Watson?"

"Certainly," I answered.

"Your leg will stand it?"

"Oh, yes."

"Here you are, doggy! Good old Toby! Smell it, Toby, smell it!" He pushed the handkerchief under the dog's nose. Holmes then threw the handkerchief a distance away. He fastened a thick cord to the dog's collar and led him to the foot of the water barrel. The creature instantly started to bark. He put his nose to the ground and his tail in the air and started to strain at his leash. Holmes gave him some slack. The next thing we knew we were all chasing after our unknown murderer.

Toby never hesitated or swerved. He pulled us first over the wall and onto the road. As we walked, Holmes spoke about the case.

"Do not imagine that I depend on this trail for success. It is the merest chance that one of the fellows put his foot in the creosote. I have knowledge which would have let me trace them in many different ways. But he did step in the creosote. And so this is the fastest way to find them."

"Holmes, I marvel at the means by which you have obtained results already. How, for example, could you describe the wooden-legged man so?"

"Pshaw, my dear boy! It was simplicity itself. It was all very clear. Two officers who are in command of a prison learn an important secret as to buried treasure. A map is drawn for them by an Englishman named Jonathan Small. We saw his name on the diagram found in Captain Morstan's baggage. He had signed it in behalf of himself and associates—the sign of the four, he had called it. The officers, or one of them, find the treasure with the use of this diagram. He brings it to England. Now, then, why didn't Jonathan Small or one of his friends get the treasure himself? The answer is clear. The map is dated. It was at a time when Morstan was in close contact with convicts. Jonathan Small did not get the treasure because he and his friends were themselves convicts and could not get away."

"But this is mere guesswork," said I.

"It is more than that. It is the only theory that covers the facts. Let us see how it fits with the second mystery of tonight. Major Sholto remains at peace for many years. Throughout that time he has the treasure. Then he receives a letter from India that gives him a great fright. What was that?"

"A letter that said the men he had wronged had been set free," I guessed.

"Or had escaped. That is much more likely. For Sholto would have known the term of their imprisonment. It would not have been a surprise to him. What does he do then? He guards himself against a wooden-legged man—an Englishman, mind you ... for he mistakes an English tradesman for him and actually fires a shot at him. The others are all Indians. Therefore we may say with confidence that the wooden-legged man is Jonathan Small. Does that reasoning strike you incorrect?"

"No. It is clear," said I.

"Well, then. Let us put ourselves in the place of Jonathan Small. Let us look at it from his point of view. He came to England with two ideas. One is to regain the treasure. The other is to seek revenge on the man who wronged him. He found out where Sholto lived. Perhaps he made contact with someone in the house. There is the butler, Lal Rao, whom we have not seen. Mrs. Bernstone says that he is not a very nice character. But Small could not find out where the treasure was hidden. No one had ever known except the Major and one servant, who was now dead. Then he learns that the Major, too, is on his deathbed. So he rushes to the house, afraid that the secret will die with him. He looks in at the window. He does not enter because the two sons are present. But his appearance frightens the Major to death.

"Later that night he enters the room. He searches through the Major's papers in the hope of finding some clue as to the treasure's whereabouts. Finally he leaves a memento of the visit of the form of a note. He probably had intended to kill the Major and leave just such a note on his body as a sign that it was not a common murder. Do you follow me?"

"Yes, indeed," I replied.

"Now, what could Jonathan Small do? He couldn't watch over the house every minute. So he makes contact with someone in the house. They are to tell him the minute the treasure is discovered. Sure enough, the discovery is made and he is told about it at once. But with his wooden leg he cannot climb up into its hiding place. And so he takes a partner. This partner accidentally steps into the creosote and here we are on a six-mile walk."

"But it was the partner, not Jonathan, who committed the murder."

"Quite so. And I don't believe Jonathan was too pleased about it either. There were marks on the floor which showed he stamped about in an angry fashion when he entered the room. He bore no grudge against Bartholomew Sholto. He would have preferred him to be bound and gagged. But he had no control over his companion. Bartholomew was dead before he entered the room. So Jonathan Small left his note, lowered the treasure and climbed down himself. That was the sequence of events, as far as I can see. As to his appearance—he had to be roughly the same age as Major Sholto and Captain Morstan. He would clearly be sunburned after serving time in such an oven as the Andamans. His height was easily figured from the length of his stride. Thaddeus Sholto was struck by the fact that he was very hairy. That is how I knew he wore a beard."

"And the partner?"

"Ah, well, there is no great mystery in that. But you will know all about it soon enough. Have you a pistol?"

"I have my stick."

"It is just possible that we may need something of the sort. I shall leave Jonathan to you. But if the other fellow turns nasty I shall shoot him dead." He took out his revolver as he spoke. He loaded two of the chambers and put it back in the pocket of his coat.

By this time we had entered the city. Laborers and dockmen were astir and strange dogs sauntered up and down. But Toby took no notice of the people or other animals. He trotted onward with his nose to the ground.

The men we were following had taken a rather zigzag path, most likely to shake anyone following them. Finally the dog began to run in circles with one ear dropped and the other cocked.

"What is the matter with the dog?" growled Holmes. "They surely would not have taken a cab or gone off in a balloon!"

"Perhaps they stood here for some time," I suggested.

"Ah! It's all right. He's off again," said my companion.

Toby had suddenly started off again. The trail now seemed hotter than ever. The dog was tugging at the leash and trying to break into a run. I could see by the gleam in Holmes' eye that he thought we were near our journey's end.

We were now outside a large timber yard. Here the dog turned down a side gate. He raced through the sawdust and shavings, down an alley, around a passage and between two woodpiles. Finally he gave a yelp and sprang upon a large barrel which stood on a handcart. The dog looked from one of us to the other excitedly. The bottom of the barrel and the wheels of the cart were smeared with a dark liquid. The whole air smelled of wood tar.

Sherlock Holmes and I looked blankly at each other. Then we burst into a fit of laughter.

Chapter 8
The Baker Street Irregulars

"What now?" I asked. "Toby has lost the scent."

"Creosote is used all over London, especially for seasoning wood. Poor Toby is not to blame."

"We must get on the main scent again," said I.

"Yes. Clearly we must go back to where the dog seemed confused. That is where the two trails crossed. We took the wrong one. Now we must follow the other."

There was no difficulty in this. We led Toby to where he had gone wrong. He smelled about in a circle and then dashed off in a fresh direction.

"We must be careful that he does not lead us to where the creosote barrel came from," said I.

"I had thought of that," said Holmes. "But he keeps on the pavement. The barrel was pushed in the street. No, we are on the true scent now."

Toby led us right down to the water's edge where there was a small wooden wharf. He stood looking out at the water beyond.

"We are out of luck," said Holmes. "They have taken a boat here." Several small boats and punts were lying about in the water. We took Toby around to each in turn but he made no sign.

There was a small brick house near the landing. A wooden sign hung in one of the windows. "Mordecai

Smith" was printed across it in large letters. Underneath it said: "Boats to hire by the hour or day." Another sign said that they had a steam-powered boat for rent as well.

Just then a little, curly-headed lad came running out. He was followed by a plump, red-faced woman with a large sponge in her hand.

"You come back and be washed, Jack," she shouted. "Come back, you young imp. If your father comes home and finds you like that he'll be angry!"

"Dear little chap!" said Holmes. "What a fine child, Mrs. Smith!"

"Lord bless you, sir. He is that. He can be almost too much for me to manage, especially when my man is away for days at a time."

"Away is he?" said Holmes in a disappointed voice. "I am sorry for that. I wanted to speak with Mr. Smith!"

"He's been away since yesterday morning, sir. To tell the truth, I'm beginning to feel frightened about him. But if it was about the boat, maybe I can help you."

"I wanted to hire his steamboat," said Holmes.

"Why, bless you, sir. That's what he's in right now. That's what puzzles me. I know there ain't enough coals in her to take her far. And what good is a steamboat without coals to make steam? He should have been back by now."

"Perhaps he bought some coal at a wharf down the river."

"He might, but it's not like him. Besides, I don't like that wooden-legged man with his ugly face and crazy talk."

"A wooden-legged man?" said Holmes blandly.

"Yes, sir. He was a brown, monkey-faced chap. He's

come by more than once. He came up early yesterday morning. What's more, my man knew he was coming. He had already steamed up the boat. I tell you straight, I don't feel easy about it."

"But, my dear Mrs. Smith," said Holmes. "You are frightening yourself about nothing. How can you be so sure it was the wooden-legged man?"

"His voice, sir. I knew his voice. It is thick and foggy. He tapped at the window—about three in the morning. 'Hurry up, matey, shake a leg.' My man woke up Jim—that's my eldest. And away they went without so much as a word to me. I could hear the wooden leg clacking on the stones."

"And was this wooden-legged man alone?" Holmes asked.

"Couldn't say. I didn't hear no one else."

"I am sorry, Mrs. Smith. I wanted a steam-boat . . . and I have heard good reports of the—let me see, what is her name?"

"The *Aurora*, sir."

"Ah! She's not that old green boat with a yellow line—very broad in the beam?"

"No, indeed. She's as trim a little thing as any on the river. She's been fresh painted—black with red stripes."

"Thanks. I hope that you will hear soon from Mr. Smith. I am going down the river. If I should see anything of the *Aurora* I shall let him know that you are uneasy. A black funnel, you say?"

"Black with a white band," said Mrs. Smith.

"Ah, of course. Good morning, Mrs. Smith."

We started to walk away.

"The main thing with people is never to let them

think that their information is important to you. If you do, they will instantly shut up like an oyster," said Holmes.

"Our course now seems pretty clear," I said.

"What would you do, then?"

"I would hire a boat and go down the river after the *Aurora.*"

"My dear fellow, it would be a colossal task. She may have stopped at any wharf along the river. Below the bridge there is a maze of landing places. It would take you days and days to check them out on your own."

"Employ the police, then?"

"No, I shall probably call Athelney Jones in at the last minute. He is not a bad fellow, and I should not like to do anything to injure him professionally. But I want to work this case out myself."

"Could we advertise, asking for information?"

"Worse and worse! Our men would know that we are hot on their heels. They would leave the country in an instant. They are likely to leave as it is. But if they think they are safe, they will not be in such a hurry. Jones will be of use to us there. His view of the case is sure to be in the papers. It will make the runaways think that everyone is off on the wrong scent."

"What are we to do, then?" I asked.

"Take this cab and drive home. We'll have some breakfast and get an hour's sleep. I am quite sure we'll be up late tonight as well. Stop at a post office, cabby! We will keep Toby. He may be of use to us yet."

We pulled up at the post office and Holmes sent his telegram. "Whom do you think it was to?" he asked as we continued on.

"I am sure I don't know," said I.

"Do you remember the Baker Street division of the detective police force? I used them on the Jefferson Hope case."

"You mean that gang of street youths? Yes, I remember them well," I said laughing.

"This is just the case for them. If they fail me, I have other ideas. But I shall try them first. That wire is to their leader, Wiggins."

It was between eight and nine o'clock now. I was limp and weary from being up the entire night. But a bath at Baker Street and a complete change of clothes freshened me up wonderfully. When I came down to the sitting room I found the breakfast laid and Holmes pouring out the coffee.

"Here it is," said he, laughing. He pointed to an open newspaper. "Jones has made his views very clear. But you have had enough of the case. Better have your ham and eggs first."

I took the paper from him and read the article, "Mysterious Business at Upper Norwood:"

About twelve o'clock last night Mr. Bartholomew Sholto, of Pondicherry Lodge, Upper Norwood, was found dead in his room. The circumstances point to foul play. No actual traces of violence can be found on Mr. Sholto's body. A valuable collection of gems, however, has been carried off. The discovery was first made by Mr. Sherlock Holmes and Dr. Watson. They had called at the house with the victim's brother, Mr. Thaddeus Sholto. Mr. Athelney

Jones, the well-known police detective, happened to be at Norwood Police Station. He was at the scene of the crime within a half-hour of the alarm. His fine skill as a detective led to the immediate arrest of Mr. Thaddeus Sholto, the housekeeper, Mrs. Bernstone, an Indian butler named Lal Rao, and a porter or gatekeeper, named McMurdo. The prompt and energetic action of Athelney Jones once again shows the superior quality of our force.

"Isn't it gorgeous!" said Holmes. "What do you think of it?"

"Jones has arrested everyone in sight. I think we are lucky to still be free!"

"So do I."

At this moment there was a loud ring at the bell. I could hear Mrs. Hudson, our landlady. Her voice was raised in dismay.

"By heaven, Holmes," I said. "I believe they are really after us!"

"No, it's not quite so bad as that. It's my own unofficial police force—the Baker Street Irregulars."

There was a pattering of bare feet on the stairs. In rushed a dozen dirty and ragged street youths. They instantly drew up in line and stood quietly facing us. The tallest and eldest one stepped forward.

"Got your message, sir," said he, "and brought 'em sharp."

"In future they can report to you, Wiggins, and you to me. I cannot have the home invaded in this way. However, it is just as well this once. It is better for you all to hear my instructions. I want to find the whereabouts of a steamboat called the *Aurora*, owner Mordecai Smith, black with two red stripes, funnel black with a white band. She is downriver somewhere. I want one boy to be at Mordecai Smith's to say if the boat comes back. You must divide the task among yourselves and check both sides of the river thoroughly. Let me know the moment you have news. Is that all clear?"

"Yes, sir," said Wiggins.

"The old scale of pay, and a bonus to the boy who finds the boat. Here's a day in advance. Now off you go!" He handed them a coin each. Away they buzzed down the stairs and out onto the street.

"If the boat is above water they will find her," said Holmes. He rose from the table and lit his pipe.

"They can go everywhere, see everything, overhear everyone. I expect to hear before evening that they have spotted her. In the meanwhile, we can do nothing but wait. We cannot pick up the broken trail until we find either the *Aurora* or Mr. Mordecai Smith."

"Are you going to bed, Holmes?" I asked.

"No, I am not tired. I never feel tired by work, though idleness exhausts me completely. I am going to smoke and to think over this queer business. Wooden-legged men are not so common, and the other man in the case is absolutely unique!"

"That other man again!"

"I have no wish to make a mystery of him—to you, anyway. You must have formed some opinion. Now, do consider the information. Small footprints, toes never tightened by boots, bare feet, a stone-headed weapon, small pointed darts. What do you make of all this?"

"A savage!" I exclaimed. "Perhaps one of those Indian men whose names are next to 'the sign of the four.'"

"When I first saw signs of strange weapons I thought so. But then I saw the footprints. The three names are all Hindu or Moslem. They are all from the mainland. Mainland India has its share of small men, but none could have left such marks as that. These little darts, too, could only be shot in one way. They are from a blowpipe. Now, then, where are we to find our savage?"

"South America," I guessed.

He stretched up his hand and took a bulky book from the shelf. "What have we here? 'Andaman Islands, situated 340 miles to the north of Sumatra, in the Bay of Bengal, belonging to India.' Hum! Hum! Ah, here we are. 'The natives of the Andaman Islands may perhaps claim the distinction of being the smallest race upon this earth. The average height is rather below four feet, although many full-grown adults may be found who are very much smaller than this. Their feet and hands are remarkably small. They are a savage people and have always been hostile to visitors to their land. They have been known to brain them with their stone-headed clubs or shoot them with their poisoned arrows. Their massacres always conclude in a cannibal feast.' Nice friendly people, Watson! If this fellow had been left on his own this affair might have turned out even more devilish than it is!"

"How did Jonathan Small get such a strange companion?"

"Ah, that I cannot say. Since we already knew that

Small was in the Andaman Islands, it was not so very great to deduce that this fellow came from there as well. No doubt we shall learn more in time," said Holmes. "Lie down there on the sofa and see if I can put you to sleep."

He took up his violin from the corner. As I stretched myself out, he began to play. I vaguely remember seeing his long limbs, his serious face, the rise and fall of the violin bow. Then I seemed to be floating away upon a soft sea of sound, until I found myself in dreamland with the sweet face of Mary Morstan looking down upon me.

Chapter 9
A Break in the Chain

It was late in the afternoon before I woke. Sherlock Holmes still sat exactly as I had left him. The only thing that had changed was that he had laid aside his violin, and was now reading a book. He looked across at me as I stirred. I noticed that his face was dark and troubled.

"You have slept soundly," he said. "I feared that our talk would wake you."

"I heard nothing," I answered. "Have you had fresh news then?"

"Unfortunately, no. I confess that I am surprised and disappointed. I expected something definite by this time. Wiggins has just been up to report. He says they have found no trace of the boat. It is very annoying, as time is precious."

"Can I do anything? I am perfectly fresh now and quite ready for another night's outing."

"No, we can do nothing. We can only wait. If we go ourselves, the message might come while we were away. This would only delay matters. You can do what you will, but I must remain on guard."

"Then I shall run over to Camberwell and call upon Mrs. Cecil Forrester. She asked me to, yesterday."

"On Mrs. Cecil Forrester?" asked Holmes. There was a twinkle in his eyes.

"Well, of course, on Miss Morstan, too. They were anxious to hear what had happened. I shall be back in an hour or two," I remarked.

"All right. Good luck! But, I say, since you are going that way, would you return Toby as well? I don't think we'll have any use for him."

I took the dog and left him with his owner. Then I went to Camberwell. I found Miss Morstan a little weary after her night's adventure, but very eager to hear the news. Mrs. Forrester, too, was full of curiosity. I told them all that we had done, although I left out the most dreadful parts of the tragedy. I spoke of Mr. Sholto's death, but I said nothing of the exact manner of it. Still, they were startled and amazed.

"It is a romance!" cried Mrs. Forrester. "A wronged lady, half a million in treasure, a cannibal, and a wooden-legged villain. Much more interesting than a dragon or a wicked earl."

"Yes, we even have two knights to the rescue!" added Miss Morstan, with a bright glance to me.

"Why, Mary, your fortune depends on the outcome of this mystery. I don't think you are nearly excited enough. Just imagine what it must be like to be so rich and to have the world at your feet," said Mrs. Forrester.

Miss Morstan tossed her head as though she cared little for such riches.

"It is for Mr. Thaddeus Sholto that I am anxious," she said. "Nothing else truly matters right now. I think he has behaved most kindly and honorably throughout. It is our duty to clear him of this dreadful and unfounded charge."

It was evening by the time I left Camberwell, and

quite dark by the time I reached home. My companion's book and pipe lay by his chair, but he had disappeared. I looked about in the hope of seeing a note, but there was none.

"Has Mr. Sherlock Holmes gone out?" I asked Mrs. Hudson.

"No, sir. He has gone to his room. Do you know, sir," she lowered her voice, "I am afraid for his health."

"Why so, Mrs. Hudson?"

"Well, he's acting so strange, sir. After you left he walked and walked up and down, up and down. Then I heard him talking to himself and muttering. Every time the bell rang he came out onto the stair and asked, 'What is that, Mrs. Hudson?' And now he has slammed off to his room. I hope he's not going to be ill, sir. I suggested he take some medicine, but he gave me such a look that I ran from the room."

"I don't think that you have any cause to be uneasy, Mrs. Hudson," I answered. "I have seen him like this before. He has some small matter on his mind. It is making him restless." I tried to speak lightly to our landlady. But that night I grew uneasy myself. All night I could hear the dull sound of his pacing back and forth, back and forth.

At breakfast time he looked worn and haggard.

"You are making yourself sick, old man," I remarked. "I heard you marching about last night."

"I could not sleep," he answered. "This problem is gnawing at me. I know the man, the boat, everything and yet I can get no news. I have set other sources to work. I have used every means of getting information. The whole river has been searched on either side. But still there is no news, nor has Mrs. Smith heard from her husband. I am beginning to think they sunk!"

"Or Mrs. Smith put us on the wrong scent," I said.

"No, I think that idea can be dismissed. I made inquiries, and there is a boat of that description."

"Could it have gone up the river?" I asked.

"I have considered that possibility too. There is a search party who will look into it. If no news comes today, I shall start off myself tomorrow. But surely we shall hear something."

We did not, however. No word came to us either from Wiggins or any other source. All day we waited for news and yet none came. By nightfall Holmes could not be spoken to. He busied himself preparing chemicals, the smell of which nearly drove me from the apartment. At last I went to bed, while Holmes remained with his test tubes.

In the early dawn I woke with a start. There was Sherlock Holmes standing at my bedside. He was dressed like a sailor with a pea jacket and a red scarf around his neck.

"I am off down the river, Watson," said he. "I have been turning the matter over in my mind. I can see only one way out of it. It is worth trying at least."

"Surely I can come with you, then?" said I.

"No. You can be much more useful if you remain here. Some message still may come. I want you to open all notes and telegrams and act in whatever way you see fit. I am afraid you will not be able to wire me as I do not know precisely where I am going. But I hope not to be gone long."

I had heard nothing of him by breakfast time. On

opening the newspaper I found another article on the matter. "The Norwood Tragedy," the headline read.

We have reason to believe that the matter is more mysterious and complex than originally thought. Fresh evidence has shown that it is quite impossible that Mr. Thaddeus Sholto could have been in any way concerned in the matter. He and the housekeeper, Mrs. Bernstone, were released yesterday evening. It is believed, however, that the police have a clue as to the real culprits. Further arrests are expected any moment.

"Well, at least our friend Sholto is safe," I thought and tossed the paper down onto the table. Just then my eye caught an advertisement lower on the page. It ran this way:

LOST—Mordecai Smith, boatman, and his son, Jim, left Smith's wharf at or about three o'clock last Tuesday morning. They were in the steamboat, *Aurora*, black with two red stripes, funnel black with a white band. A reward will be paid to anyone who can give information to Mrs. Smith at Smith's wharf or at 221B Baker Street.

This was clearly Holmes' work. The Baker Street address proved that. It struck me rather clever. If the runaways saw it they would see in it nothing more than an anxious wife looking for her husband.

It was a long day. Every time there was a knock at the door I jumped. I was sure it was either Holmes or an answer to his advertisement.

At three o'clock in the afternoon there was a loud peal of the bell. To my surprise it was none other than Mr. Athelney Jones. He had changed greatly from the confident detective of the other night. Now he was downcast and meek.

"Good day, sir, good day," said he. "Mr. Sherlock Holmes is out, I understand."

"Yes. I am not sure when he will be back. Perhaps you would care to wait. Take that chair and try one of these cigars."

"Thank you. I don't mind if I do," said he.

"And a whiskey and soda?"

"Well, half a glass. It is very hot this time of year. I have had a good deal to worry and try me. You know my theory about the Norwood case?"

"I remember that you expressed one," said I.

"Well, I have had time to reconsider it. I had my net drawn tightly around Mr. Sholto. Then pop! He went through a hole in the middle of it. He was able to prove where he was at the time of the murder. From the time that he left his brother's room he was never out of sight of someone or other. So it could not be he who climbed over roofs and through trapdoors. It's a very dark case. My professional credit is at stake. I should be very glad of assistance."

"We all need help sometimes," said I.

"Your friend Mr. Sherlock Holmes is a wonderful man, sir," said he. "I have seen him work on many cases.

He has always been able to shed some light on them. He is irregular in his methods and a little quick in jumping to theories. But on the whole, I think he would have made a good police officer. I don't care who knows it. I received a wire from him this morning. In it he says he has a clue to this Sholto business. Here is his message."

He took the telegram out of his pocket and handed it to me. "Go to Baker Street at once," it said. "If I have not returned, wait for me. I am close on the track of the Sholto gang. You can come with us tonight if you want to be in at the finish."

"This sounds good," I said. "He has picked up the scent again."

"Ah, then he has had problems too," exclaimed Jones. "Even the best of us get thrown off sometimes. Of course this may be a false alarm. Still, it is my duty as an officer of the law to follow all leads. But there is someone at the door. Perhaps it is he."

A heavy step was heard up the stair. The man was wheezing as though he was terribly out of breath. He entered the room slowly. He was an aged man, in seafaring dress with an old peajacket buttoned up to his throat. His back was bent, his knees were shaky and his breathing was heavy. He had a colored scarf around his neck. I could see little of his face except his dark eyes and white bushy brows.

"What is it, my man?" I asked.

"Is Mr. Sherlock Holmes here?" said he.

"No, but I am acting for him. You can tell me any message you have for him. Was it about Mordecai Smith's boat?"

"Yes, I knows well where it is. An' I knows where the men he is after are. An' I knows where the treasure is. I knows all about it."

"Then tell me, and I shall let him know."

"It was him I was to tell it," he repeated.

"Well, you must wait for him."

"No, no, I ain't goin' to lose a whole day to please no one. If Mr. Holmes ain't here, then Mr. Holmes must find it all out for himself. I don't care about the look of either of you, and I won't tell a word."

He shuffled toward the door, but Athelney Jones got in front of him.

"Wait a bit, friend," said he. "You have important information. You must not walk off. We shall keep you, whether you like it or not until our friend returns."

The old man made a slow run toward the door, but Jones put his broad back against it.

"Pretty sort o' treatment this!" he cried. "I come here to see a gentleman . . . and you two seize me and treat me like this!"

"Sit over here and you will not have long to wait."

He sat down in the armchair and wearily rested his face in his hands. Jones and I resumed our cigars and our talk. Then suddenly Holmes' voice broke in upon us.

"I think that you might offer me a cigar too," he said.

We both jumped in our chairs. There was Holmes sitting close to us.

"Holmes!" I exclaimed. "You here! But where is the old man?"

"Here is the old man," said he. He held out a heap of white hair. "Here he is—wig, whiskers, eyebrows, and all. I thought my disguise was pretty good, but I hardly expected it to fool you!"

"Ah, you rogue!" cried Jones, highly delighted. "You would have made a rare actor. I thought I knew the glint in your eye. You didn't fool us so easily."

"I have been working in that getup all day," said Sherlock Holmes. "You see, a good many criminals now know me. Especially after our friend here took to writing about my cases. I can only go on the warpath under some simple disguise like this. You got my wire?"

"Yes, that is what brought me here," answered Jones.

"How has your case gone?"

"It has all come to nothing. I have had to release two of my prisoners, and there is no evidence against the other two."

"Never mind. We shall give you two others in their place. You are welcome to all the official credit, but you must act as I tell you. Is that agreed?"

"Entirely, if you will turn over the men to me."

"Well, then, I shall need a fast police boat—a steam-powered one. It is to be at the dock at seven o'clock."

"That is easily done. One is always there," replied Athelney Jones.

"And I shall want two strong men—in case of difficulties."

"There will be two or three in the boat. What else?"

"When we capture the men we shall get the treasure. Half of it rightfully belongs to Miss Morstan. I would like my friend, Watson, to take it to her. Let her be the first to open the chest. Eh, Watson?"

"It would be a great pleasure to me," I said.

"That's rather unusual," said Jones. "However this whole case is unusual. I suppose we can look the other way. But the treasure must afterward be handed over to the police until there is an official investigation."

"Certainly. That can easily be done. One other point. I should like to hear a few details from the lips of Jonathan Small himself. I want to have an interview with him . . . either here in my rooms or elsewhere."

"Well, you are in charge now. I have had no proof of the existence of this Jonathan Small. However, if you catch him, I don't see how I can refuse you an interview with him."

"Then it is understood?" asked Holmes.

"Perfectly. Is there anything else?"

"Only that you dine with us. Dinner will be ready in half an hour. I am preparing it myself. Watson, you didn't know that cooking was one of my many skills."

Chapter 10
The End of the Islander

Our meal was a merry one. Holmes appeared to be in an exceptionally good mood. After the meal Holmes poured us each a glass of sherry. "One last toast to the success of our little expedition. And now it is high time we were off. Have you a pistol, Watson?"

"I have my army revolver right here in the desk."

"You had best take it, then. I see that the cab is at the door. I ordered it for half-past six."

It was a little past seven before we reached the dock. Our police boat was waiting. Holmes looked at it carefully.

"Is there anything to mark it as a police boat?" he asked.

"Yes—that green lamp at the side."

"Then take it off."

The small change was made. We stepped on board and the ropes were cast off. Jones, Holmes, and I sat in front. There was one man at the rudder, one to tend the engines, and two burly police inspectors in the rear.

Our craft was a very fast one. We shot past long lines of loaded barges. Holmes smiled as we passed a river steamship and left her far behind.

"We ought to be able to catch anything on the river," said he.

"Well, hardly that. But there aren't many steamboats to beat us," replied Jones.

"We shall have to catch the *Aurora*. She is well-known for her speed. I will tell you what has happened, Watson. You remember how upset I was when no word came about the *Aurora*?"

"Yes."

"Well, I gave my mind a good rest by working with my chemicals. Then I went back to our problem. I thought the whole matter over again. My Baker Street boys had searched the river and found nothing. The boat was not docked somewhere, nor had it returned. I knew that Small had been in London for some time, as he had been on the lookout for the treasure. That meant that he had lodgings somewhere. There was a good chance that he would not have given them up yet. He might need them to flee to. Jonathan Small had to know his partner would easily be identified. Even in a topcoat and hat, he could not hide him. It would be best, therefore, to travel only at night. Mrs. Smith had said that they had come at 3 A.M. That meant that they did not have much time before daylight. Therefore, I believed, they had not gone far. They had paid Mr. Smith to reserve his boat for their final escape. Then they had gone back to their lodgings with the treasure chest. They would read the papers and find out what the situation was. Then they would make their way to a ship bound for some distant land."

"But the boat? They could not have taken that to their lodgings," I said.

"Quite so. Small would not have wanted to send the boat back. Nor would he want to dock it in a wharf where it could easily be found. That would put the police too easily on their trail. How could he hide the boat yet have her at hand when he wanted her? I wondered what I should do myself in his shoes. I could only think of one way of doing it. I might give the boat to a shipbuilder or repairer with directions to have some small change made. The boat would then be removed to his shed or yard. It would thus be hidden and yet I could have it at a few hours' notice."

"That seems simple enough," I agreed.

"It is just these simple things that are usually overlooked. However I was determined to see if I was right. I started out in this disguise. I inquired at all the shipyards down the river. I drew blank at fifteen, but at the sixteenth—Jacobson's—I found the *Aurora*. And I learned that she had been handed over to them by a wooden-legged man. He had given them directions to make some minor change to the rudder. 'There's nothing wrong with her rudder,' said the foreman. 'There she is, with the red stripes.'

"At that moment who should come in but Mordecai Smith. I should not have known him but he yelled out his name and the name of his boat. 'I want her tonight at eight o'clock,' said he. 'Eight o'clock sharp. I have two gentlemen who won't be kept waiting!' They had paid him well, for he was handing out coins as though he were a millionaire. I followed him some distance, but he went into a tavern. So I went back to the shipyard. On the way I saw one of my Baker Street boys. I instructed him to stand watch over the boat. He is to stand at the water's edge and wave his handkerchief to us when they start to leave. We shall be hiding under the bridge. It will be a strange thing if we do not capture men, treasure and all."

"You planned it all very neatly, whether they are the right men or not," said Jones. "But if I had been in charge, I would have had a huge number of police at Jacobson's Yard. I would have arrested them when they came to get the *Aurora*."

"Which would have been never," said Holmes. "This man Small is a pretty smart fellow. He would send a scout on ahead. If anything looked wrong he would wait another week."

"You could have followed Mordecai Smith. He would have led them to their hiding place," I suggested.

"No, I would have wasted my day. Smith does not know where they live. I am sure Small sends him messages. And why should Smith ask any questions as long as he's paid well. No, I thought over every possible course of action and this is the best."

"That is Jacobson's Yard," said Holmes. He pointed to a huge shipyard filled with masts and rigging. "Cruise gently up and down here under the cover of the bridge." He took a pair of night-binoculars from his pocket and gazed at the shore. "I see my guard at his post," he remarked, "but no sign of a handkerchief."

We waited for some time before we saw a white flutter on the shore.

"Yes, it is your boy," I cried. "I can see him plainly."

"And there is the *Aurora*!" exclaimed Holmes. "And going like the devil! Full speed ahead, engineer. Follow that boat with the yellow light. By heaven, I shall never forgive myself if she escapes us now."

She had slipped unseen through the yard entrance.
Then she had passed between two or three smaller boats.
By the time we saw her she was going at full speed. Now
she was flying down the stream, near in to the shore.
Jones looked gravely at her and shook his head.

"She is very fast," he said. "I doubt if we shall catch
her."

"We *must* catch her!" cried Holmes. "Faster, faster."

The furnaces roared and the powerful engines
whizzed and clanked. Her sharp steep prow cut through
the water and sent two rolling waves to right and left of
us. A yellow lantern cast a beam of light in front of us.
We could just see the vague outline of the *Aurora* and the
white foam she left behind. We flashed past barges,
steamers, merchant-boats, in and out, behind one and
the other. Voices hailed us out of the darkness, but the
Aurora thundered on and still we followed close upon
her track.

"Pile it on, men, pile it on!" cried Holmes. He
looked down into the engine room where the men were
filling the furnace with coals. "Get every pound of steam
you can."

"I think we are gaining on them," said Jones.

"I am sure of it," said I. "We shall catch up to her in
a few minutes."

At that very moment a tugboat passed right between
us. By the time we went around it the *Aurora* had gained
over two hundred yards. On we went, faster and faster.
Our boat shook in its supreme effort. Jones turned our
searchlight upon the *Aurora*. We could now see the
figures on her deck. One man sat in the rear. He was
stooping down over something black. Beside him lay a

dark mass. The boy held the tiller. Against the red glare of the furnace I could see old Smith. He was stripped to the waist and shoveling coals for dear life. They may have doubted that we were following them at first, but now there could be no doubt about it. We followed their every wind and turn. Steadily, we drew closer and closer to them. In the silence of the night we could hear the clanking of their machinery. Nearer and nearer we came. Jones yelled for them to stop. We were no more than four boat's lengths behind them. Both of us were flying at tremendous speeds. The man now sprang up and shook his fists at us. He was a good-sized, powerful man. A wooden stump was where his right leg should have been. Suddenly the bundle beside him straightened itself. A tiny man appeared. He was wrapped in a blanket and I could see only his face. But that was enough to give a man a sleepless night. His small eyes glared and his teeth grinned and chattered at us with animal fury.

"Fire if he raises his hand," Holmes said quietly.

We were within a boat's length of them now. Holmes had already drawn his revolver and I now whipped out mine.

Just then the savage took out a blowpipe. He put it to his lips. Our pistols rang out together. He whirled around, threw up his arms, and fell sideways into the stream. At the same moment the wooden-legged man threw himself on the rudder. He started to steer toward the shore. Meanwhile we sped past her. By the time we had turned around, the *Aurora* was up onto the mudbank. Small sprang out, but his stump sank into the wet soil. He struggled and struggled, but he could not free himself. He yelled in rage and kicked with his other leg, but he sank further and further into the soil. We brought our boat alongside the *Aurora* and lassoed our man. Then we hauled him like a fish toward us. The two Smiths, father and son, came meekly on board. A solid iron chest stood upon the deck. There could be no doubt that this was the Sholtos' treasure. There was no key but it was very heavy. We carefully transferred it to our cabin. When all were aboard, we shoved off once again. As we moved slowly upstream, we flashed our search-light in every direction. But there was no sign of the Islander. Somewhere in the dark ooze at the bottom of the river lie the bones of that strange visitor to our shores.

"See here," said Holmes as we stood on deck. He pointed to the cabin wall behind us. "We were just quick enough with our pistols!" There, sure enough, was one of those murderous darts. It must have whizzed between us as we fired.

Chapter 11
The Great Agra Treasure

Our captive was a sunburned fellow with graying hair and a full beard. He now sat with his handcuffed hands upon his lap and his head sunk upon his breast. Opposite him was the treasure chest he had so desperately wanted and lost.

"Well, Jonathan Small," said Holmes, lighting a cigar, "I am sorry that it has come to this."

"And so am I, sir," he answered frankly. "I give you my word I did not kill Mr. Sholto. It was the little Islander, Tonga, who did it. Tonga shot one of his cursed darts into him. I had no part in it, sir. I was very upset about it. I hit the fellow for doing it, but it was done and I could not undo it."

"Have a cigar," said Sherlock Holmes. "You had best have a drink out of my flask as well. You are very wet. Tell me, how did you expect the small native to overpower Mr. Sholto and hold him while you were climbing the rope?"

"You seem to know as much about it as if you were there, sir. The truth is that I hoped to find the room empty. I knew the ways of the house pretty well. It was the time Mr. Sholto usually went down to supper. I shall make no secret of this business. My best defense is the simple truth. If it had been the old Major in there I would have killed him in an instant."

"You are under the charge of Mr. Athelney Jones, of Scotland Yard. He is going to bring you to my rooms and I shall ask you for a true account of the matter. You must tell me the exact truth however. I think I can help you if you do. I am sure I can prove that the man was dead before you ever reached the room."

"That he was, sir. I never got such a turn in my life as when I saw him grinning at me with his head on his shoulder. I was so angry, I'd have half-killed the native if he hadn't scrambled off. That was how he came to leave his club and some of his darts too. That must be how you got on our scent, though how you kept on it I really don't know. It's a queer thing," he added with a bitter smile, "I have a fair claim to near half a million of money. Yet I spent half my life building a dam in the Andamans and am likely to spend the other half digging drains in England. It was an evil day for me when I first clapped eyes on that merchant Achmet and the Agra treasure. The treasure never brought anything to anyone. It brought fear and guilt to Major Sholto, it brought death to his son and to me it has meant slavery for life."

At that moment Athelney Jones came into the cabin. "Well, I think we can congratulate each other," he remarked to Holmes. "Pity we didn't capture the other alive, but there was no choice. I say, Holmes, this has worked out well."

"All is well that ends well," said Holmes. "But I certainly didn't know the *Aurora* was such a fast boat."

"Smith says she is one of the fastest boats on the

river, and if another man had been there to help with the engines we should never have caught her," said Jones. "He swears that he knew nothing of this Norwood business."

"That's true," cried our prisoner. "We told him nothing. But we paid him well and he was to get a bonus if we reached our ship, the *Esmeralda*, bound for Brazil."

"Well, if he has done no wrong we shall see that no wrong comes to him."

"We shall land you shortly, Dr. Watson," said Jones. "Then you can take the treasure chest to Miss Morstan as agreed. It is a pity there is no key so that we can look inside. You will have to break it open. Where is the key, Small?"

"At the bottom of the river," said our prisoner.

"Hum! As if you haven't made enough work for us already. However, Doctor, do be careful. Bring the box back with you to Baker Street. You will find us there before we go on to the station."

They landed me as close to my destination as possible with a friendly inspector as my guard. In a quarter of an hour we were at Mrs. Cecil Forrester's. The servant was surprised at so late a visitor. Mrs. Forrester was out for the evening and likely to be very late. Miss Morstan however was in the drawing room. So into the drawing room I went. I carried the box and left the inspector in the cab.

At the sound of my footsteps she sprang to her feet. Color rose in her cheeks.

"I heard a cab drive up," she said. "I thought Mrs. Forrester had come back very early. I never dreamed it might be you. What news have you brought me?"

"I have brought you something better than news," said I. I put the box down upon the table. I spoke cheerfully but my heart was heavy. Now that she was to be rich, she would never consider marrying me. "I have brought you something which is worth all the news in the world. I have brought you a fortune."

She glanced at the iron box. "Is that the treasure then?" she asked coolly.

"Yes, this is the great Agra treasure. Half of it is yours and half of it is Thaddeus Sholto's. There will be few young ladies richer than you in England. Isn't it glorious?"

She must have noted my lack of enthusiasm for I saw her raise her eyebrows and she looked at me curiously.

"If I have it," said she, "I owe it to you."

"No, no," I answered. "Not to me. But to my friend, Sherlock Holmes. It was his genius that found it. As it was, we very nearly lost it at the last moment."

"Please sit down and tell me all about it. Dr. Watson," said she.

I then told her the entire story—Holmes' method of search, the discovery of the *Aurora*, the appearance of Athelney Jones, our expedition in the evening, and the wild chase down the river. She listened with parted lips and shining eyes. When I spoke of the dart which narrowly missed us, she turned so white that I thought she would faint.

"It is nothing," she said. "I am all right again. It was a shock to hear that I had placed my friends in such danger!"

"That is all over," I answered. "I will tell you no

more gloomy details. Let us turn to something brighter. There is the box. I got permission to bring it straight to you so that you could be the first to see the treasure."

"It is a pretty box," she said. "This is Indian work, I suppose?"

"Yes, they are famous for their metal work."

"And so heavy," she exclaimed, trying to lift it. "The box alone must be of some value. Where is the key?"

"Small threw it into the river," I answered. "I must borrow Mrs. Forrester's poker." There was a handle on the top in the image of a sitting Buddha. Under this I thrust one end of the poker and twisted. The lock sprung open with a loud snap. With trembling fingers, I flung back the lid. We both stood gazing in astonishment. The box was empty!

No wonder it was heavy. The iron-work was two-thirds of an inch all around. It was well-made and solid like a chest made to carry things of great value. But there was not one piece of jewelry or one coin within. It was absolutely and completely empty.

"The treasure is lost," said Miss Morstan calmly.

"Thank God!" I exclaimed.

"Why do you say that?" Miss Morstan answered.

"Because you are now within my reach again," I said and took her hand. "Because I love you and because this treasure sealed my lips. Now that it is gone I can tell you how I feel. That is why I said, 'Thank God.' "

"Then I say, 'Thank God,' too," she whispered.

Someone may have lost a treasure, but I had gained one that night.

Chapter 12
The Strange Story
of Jonathan Small

I arrived at Baker Street only a short time after Holmes, Jones, and their prisoner. Holmes lounged in his armchair while Small sat opposite him with his wooden leg crossed over his good one. Jones stood restlessly in the corner. I showed them immediately the empty box. Small leaned back in his chair at the sight of it and laughed aloud.

"This is your doing, Small," said Athelney Jones, angrily.

"Yes, I have put the treasure where you shall never lay your hands upon it. It was my treasure, and I was darned if someone else was going to have it. I tell you that no living man has any right to it, unless it be three men in the Andaman prison and myself. I've acted throughout in their names. It's been the sign of the four with us all along. Well, I know that they would have wanted me to do just what I did. Better that than letting the kin of Sholto or Morstan have it. So I threw the treasure into the river. You'll find it where the key is, and where little Tonga is. When I saw that your boat was gaining on us, I threw the treasure overboard piece by piece so that you could never get it back. I spent twenty long years in that prison. That is how I earned the Agra treasure. It was mine to throw away."

"You forget that we know nothing of all this," said Sherlock quietly. "We have not yet heard your story."

"Well, sir, if you want to hear my story I have no wish to hold back. I shall tell you God's truth, that I promise.

"I'm from Worcester originally. I was always the black sheep of the family. I never did well in school.

"I got into some trouble when I was eighteen and so joined the army bound for India. It turned out that I wasn't much good at soldiering either. I had learned how to march and to handle a musket when I was fool enough to go swimming in the Ganges. Luckily for me my company sergeant was in the water at the same time and he was a fine swimmer. A crocodile came up to me when I was halfway across the river. He nipped off my right leg, just above the knee. The sergeant swam out and dragged me to safety. I was five months in the hospital. When I was finally able to leave, I had this wooden leg strapped to my stump. I was discharged from the army as an invalid.

"I worked at a plantation for a short time afterward. But then the great mutiny broke out. There were rebels everywhere, attacking British settlements and forts. The country was turned upside down overnight. There were still many Indians loyal to the British, but any way you looked at it we were outnumbered. Everywhere women, children, and men were being killed. I joined a volunteer army, wooden leg and all. I was assigned to act as guard at the old fort of Agra. The fort was enormous. Its modern quarter was where the troops, women, and children stayed, while the old quarter was deserted. It was full of empty halls, winding passages, and long twisting corridors.

"The river washes against the front of the old fort and protects it. But on the sides and behind there are many doors. These all had to be guarded, both in the modern section and the old. We were shorthanded. It was therefore impossible to have a man at every post. So instead there was a central guardhouse in the middle of the fort and several scattered guardposts. Each one was made up of one Englishman and two loyal Indians. I was selected to stand guard at night over a door in the old section. I was instructed to fire my musket if anything went wrong, and someone from the central guardhouse would come right away. But the guardhouse was two hundred paces away, through winding passages and long corridors. I had great doubts whether they could arrive in time in case of an actual attack.

"Well, for two nights I kept watch with two fierce-looking chaps named Mahomet Singh and Abdullah Khan. They could speak English pretty well but they would not say much to me.

"The third night of my watch was dark and rainy. It was dreary work standing by that door hour after hour. I tried again and again to get the Indians to speak with me, but they would not. So I took out my pipe and laid down my musket to strike a match. In an instant the two fellows were upon me. One of them snatched up my musket and pointed it at my head. The other held a great knife to my throat. He swore that if I moved he would plunge it into me.

"My first thought was that these fellows were in

league with the rebels. I knew that if this door fell the whole fort would be lost. And so I opened my mouth to give a warning. The man who held me seemed to know my thoughts. He whispered, 'Don't make a noise. The fort is safe enough. There are no rebels on this side of the river.' There was the ring of truth in what he said. I knew if I raised my voice I'd be a dead man. So I waited in silence to see what they wanted of me.

" 'Listen to me,' said the taller and fiercer of the pair. 'You must either be with us or you must be silenced forever. Which is it to be, life or death? We can only give you three minutes to decide. Time is passing and all must be done before the changing of the guard.'

" 'How can I decide?' said I. 'You have not told me what you want of me. If it is anything against the safety of the fort you can kill me now.'

" 'It is nothing against the fort,' said he. 'Your countrymen came to India to get rich. We are only asking you to get rich too. If you join us now you shall have a share of the loot. A quarter of the treasure shall be yours.'

" 'What treasure?' I asked. 'I am as ready as the next one to be rich.'

" 'You must first swear not to raise a hand or speak a word against us. If you swear, then you shall have a quarter of the treasure. It will be equally divided among the four of us.'

" 'But we are three,' said I.

" 'No; Dost Akbar must have his share. We can tell you the tale while we await him. There is a rajah in the north who has much wealth. When the mutiny broke out he decided to divide it, in case it should be taken from him. He locked his silver and gold into his palace vaults. He placed his jewels in an iron box. This box he gave to a trusty servant to bury in the fort of Agra.

" 'This servant has disguised himself as a merchant. He is now in the city and desires to enter the fort. He is traveling with my foster brother, Dost Akbar. Dost Akbar knows his secret and has promised to lead him into the fort tonight. He plans to enter by this door. He will come soon. And he will find Mahomet Singh and myself in wait. The place is lonely and none shall know of his coming. The world shall know of the merchant Achmet no more. But the great treasure of the rajah shall be divided among us. What say you now?'

"In England the life of a man seems a great and a sacred thing. But it is different when fire and blood is all around you and you have seen death at every turn. Whether Achmet lived or died was of no importance to me. But to come home rich and show the folks that I had become a man of importance. Well, that was another thing. So I agreed to go along with them.

"Suddenly there was the glint of a shaded lantern in the distance. It was coming our way.

" 'Here they are!' I exclaimed.

" 'You will challenge him as usual,' whispered Abdullah. 'Give him no cause to fear. Send us into the fort with him. We shall do the rest while you stay on guard. Have the lantern ready to uncover so that we may be sure that it is indeed the man.'

"I could see two dark figures on the other side of the moat. I let them scramble down the sloping bank, splash through the water halfway up to the door. Then I challenged them.

" 'Who goes there?' said I.

" 'Friends,' came the answer. I uncovered my lantern and threw a flood of light upon them. The first was a tall fellow with a black beard. The other was a little, fat, round man, with a great yellow turban. He carried a bundle in his hand. It was covered by a shawl. He seemed all aquiver with fear. His hands shook and he kept looking nervously to the left and right. It gave me chills to think of killing him. But then I thought of the treasure and my heart turned cold.

" 'Your protection,' he panted, 'protection for the unhappy merchant Achmet. I have traveled a long way to seek the shelter of the fort at Agra. I have been robbed and beaten because I am a friend of the English. It is a blessed night when I am once more in safety—I and my poor possessions.'

" 'What have you in the bundle?' I asked.

" 'An iron box,' he answered. 'It contains one or two family belongings. They are of no value to others, but I would be sorry to lose them. I am not a beggar. I shall reward you and your commander, if you give me the shelter I ask.'

"I could not trust myself to speak any longer with the man. The more I looked at his fat, frightened face, the harder it seemed to slay him in cold blood. It was best to get it over.

" 'Take him to the main guard,' said I. Singh and Khan closed in upon him on each side and the tall man walked behind. I remained at the gate with the lantern.

"I could hear the sound of their footsteps along the empty corridors. Suddenly it stopped. I heard voices and a scuffle and the sound of blows. A moment later there came a rush of footsteps in my direction. I turned my lantern toward the corridor. The fat man was running toward me! There was blood smeared across his face. Close at his heels came the tall, black-bearded man. He had a knife flashing in his hand. I have never seen a man run so fast as that little merchant. I could see that if he got passed me he could save himself. For a moment my heart softened again. Then I thought of the treasure. I thrust my musket in between his legs and he went rolling twice over like a rabbit. In a second the giant was upon him and the knife was in his side. The man never uttered a moan or moved a muscle. He simply lay where he had fallen. I think myself that he may have broken his neck in the fall. You see, gentlemen, I am keeping my promise. I am telling you every word of the business, just as it happened—whether it is in my favor or not.

"Well, we carried him in, Abdullah, Akbar, and I. A fine weight he was too. Mahomet Singh was left to guard the door. We took him to where a winding passage leads to a great empty hall. The earth floor had sunk in at one place and made a natural grave. So we laid the merchant there and covered him with loose bricks. This done, we all went back to the treasure.

"It lay where he had dropped it when he was first attacked. The box was the same which now lies open upon your table. A key hung by a silken cord to that carved handle upon the top. We opened it. In the light of the lantern we could see the treasure. The gems within were blinding in their brilliance. There were one hundred and forty-three diamonds, ninety-seven very fine emeralds, one hundred and seventy rubies, forty carbuncles, two hundred and ten sapphires, sixty-one agates, and a great quantity of beryls, onyxes, cat's eyes, turquoises, and other stones. Besides this, there were nearly three hundred very fine pearls. Twelve were set in a gold necklace. By the way, this necklace had been taken out of the chest when I finally recovered it.

"After we counted our treasure, we put it back in the box. Then we carried it to the door to show Mahomet Singh. After that we vowed to stand by each other and be true to our secret. We agreed to hide our loot in a safe place until the country was at peace again. At that time we would divide it between ourselves. There was no use in dividing it now. If we were found to have such gems on us, it would cause suspicion at once. So we carried the box to the same hall where we had buried the body. We buried it behind the bricks of a wall. We made a careful note of the place. Next day I drew four plans, one for each of us. I put the sign of the four of us at the bottom. We had sworn that we should always act for all. That is an oath that I have never broken.

"Well, the rebels were soon put down by the English. Peace seemed to be returning to the country. The four of us were beginning to think it was safe to get the treasure. But then our hopes were shattered. We were arrested for the murder of the merchant Achmet.

"What happened was this. The rajah had given the jewels to Achmet because he knew he was a trusty man. But they are suspicious folk in the East. He had a second, even more trusty servant, spy upon him. This second man never let Achmet out of his sight. He saw him go into the fort with Dost Akbar. He applied for admission to the fort the next day. When he didn't find Achmet there he went to one of the commanders. A thorough

search was made and the body was found. We were all four seized and brought to trial for murder—the three of us because we guarded the door that night, and Akbar because he was with the merchant. Not a word about the jewels came out at the trial. I heard that the rajah had been ordered out of the country—outlawed. It seemed that no one knew about the treasure—or cared. All four of us were sentenced to life imprisonment. We were shipped out to Blair Island in the Andamans. Our treasure remained buried in the old fort at Agra.

"Blair Island was a hellish place. It was full of wild cannibals who would blow a poisoned dart at you in a second. I was one of the few Englishmen in camp and so received rather special treatment. After a while I was even given a small hut of my own. Of course, I was always on the lookout for some way to escape. But we were hundreds of miles from any other land.

"I spent part of my time mixing drugs for the camp surgeon. In the evenings he and his fellow officers played cards. Two of the officers were Major Sholto and Captain Morstan. Major Sholto used to lose. After a while, he grew seriously in debt.

"One night he lost even more heavily than usual. I was sitting in my hut when he and Captain Morstan came stumbling along. They were good friends and never apart. The Major was raving about his losses.

" 'I am a ruined man,' I heard him say.

" 'Nonsense, old man,' said Morstan. 'I haven't done well myself but—' That was all I could hear. But it set me to thinking.

"A couple of days later, Major Sholto was strolling on the beach. I took the chance to speak with him.

" 'I wish your advice, Major,' said I.

" 'Well, Small, what is it?' he asked.

" 'I wanted to ask you, sir,' said I. 'Who is the proper person to speak to about hidden treasure. I know where half a million lies. Since I cannot use it myself I thought I should turn it over to the authorities. Perhaps they would get my sentence shortened . . .'

" 'Half a million, Small?' he gasped.

" 'Quite that, sir—in jewels and pearls. It lies ready for anyone. And the queer thing is that the real owner is outlawed and cannot hold property, so that it belongs to the first comer.'

" 'You should give it to the government,' he stammered. '—to the government.' But I could see that he had taken the bait.

" 'You think, then, sir, that I should give the information to the Governor-General?' I said quietly.

" 'Well, well, you must not do anything rash. Let me hear all about it, Small. Give me the facts.'

"So I told him the whole story. But I made little changes so that he could not tell where it had taken place. When I finished he told me not to tell anyone and that he would see me soon.

"Two nights later he came back with his friend, Captain Morstan.

" 'I want you to let Captain Morstan hear that story from your own lips, Small,' said he.

"Well, the next thing I knew they were asking what I wanted for the treasure. They wanted to make some sort of deal.

" 'Why, there is only one bargain which a man in my position can make,' I told them. 'I shall want you to help me to my freedom, and to help my three friends to theirs. We shall then take you into partnership. We will give you a fifth share to divide between you.'

" 'Hum!' said he. 'A fifth share! That is not very tempting.'

" 'It would come to fifty thousand apiece,' said I.

" 'But how can we gain your freedom? You know that is an impossibility.'

" 'Nothing of the sort,' I answered. 'I have thought it all out to the last detail. There is only one thing stopping an escape. I have no boat fit for such a long journey and no provisions to last us for so long a time. We can arrange to board her at night. No one will see us.'

" 'It would be easier if it was just you.'

" 'None or all,' I answered. 'We have sworn it. The four of us must always act together.'

" 'Well, Small,' said the Major. 'We must first test the truth of your story. Tell me where the box is hid. I shall get a leave and go back to India in the monthly relief-boat. I can inquire into the affair.'

" 'Not so fast,' said I. 'I must have the consent of my three comrades. I tell you that it is four or none with us.'

"So we had a meeting with Mahomet Singh, Abdullah Khan, and Dost Akbar. We talked the matter over and at last came to an arrangement. We were to give the officers each a chart of that part of the Agra fort and mark the place in the wall where the treasure was hid. Major Sholto was to go to India to test our story. If he found the box he was to leave it there. He was to send a small yacht to a nearby island with provisions for our trip. Then he was to return to his duties. A little later Captain Morstan would apply for a leave and meet us at

Agra. There we would divide the treasure. Morstan would take the Major's share as well as his own. All this we sealed by the most solemn oaths. I sat up all night with paper and ink. By morning I had the two charts all ready. Each we signed with the sign of the four—that is, of Abdullah, Akbar, Mahomet, and myself.

"Well, that villain Sholto went to India, but he never came back. Captain Morstan showed me his name among a list of mailboat passengers bound for England. His uncle had died and left him a fortune. So he had left the army. But still he stole the treasure and betrayed us! Morstan went to Agra. He found that the treasure was indeed gone. That scoundrel had stolen it without carrying out any of the conditions we had agreed upon. From that day I lived only for vengeance. I thought about it day and night. It became an overpowering passion with me. I cared nothing for the law, nothing for the gallows. To escape, to track Sholto down, to have my hand at his throat—that was my only thought. Even the Agra treasure was not as important as the slaying of Sholto.

"Well, one day when the surgeon was out a little Islander was found in the woods. He was sick to death and had gone to a lonely place to die. I took him in and after a couple of months he was all right. He took a fancy to me and would not go back into the woods. I learned a little of his lingo from him and this made him even more fond of me.

"Tonga—that was his name—was a fine boatman and owned a big, roomy canoe of his own. Here was my chance to escape. I talked it over with him. He was to bring his boat around to an old unused wharf on a certain night. There he was to pick me up. I gave him directions to have aboard water, yams, coconuts and sweet potatoes.

"He was staunch and true, was little Tonga. No man ever had a more faithful mate. At the night named, he had his boat at the wharf. Tonga had brought all his belongings with him, including his blowpipe and darts. Among other things he had some matting which I made into a sort of sail. For ten days we drifted at sea. Then we were picked up by cargo boat.

"Well, we traveled all about and it took us a long time to get to England. But we finally did. I found out where Sholto lived and made friends with someone who could help me—I name no names. From him I learned that Sholto still had the jewels. Then I tried to get at him in many ways. But he was pretty sly. He had always two prizefighters, his sons, and his servants guarding over him.

"One day, however, I got word that he was dying. I hurried at once to the garden. I looked through his window. There he was with his sons beside him. I'd have gone in but just then his jaw dropped and I knew that he was gone. I got into his room that night though. I searched his papers to see if there was any record of where he had hidden the jewels. But I found nothing. Before I left I thought of my friends in the Andamans. I thought how satisfying it would be to leave some mark of our hatred. So I scrawled the sign of the four of us and pinned it to his chest. At least he would take to the grave some sign that he had robbed and befooled us.

"We earned a living by my showing poor Tonga at fairs as a cannibal. He would eat raw meat and dance his war dance. I still heard all the news at Pondicherry Lodge. For some years there was no news except that they were hunting for the treasure. But at last we heard that the treasure had been found. It was up at the top of the house, in Mr. Bartholomew's chemical laboratory. I came at once and had a look at the place. I did not see how, with my wooden leg, I was going to make my way up to it. I learned, however, that there was a trapdoor in the roof, and also about Mr. Sholto's supper hour. It seemed that I could manage the thing through Tonga. I brought him out with me with a long rope wound around his waist. He could climb like a cat. He soon made his way through the roof. But Bartholomew was still in his room. Tonga thought he had done something clever in killing him. I found him strutting about as proud as a peacock. He was very much surprised when I cursed him for being a blood-thirsty imp. I took the treasure box, let it down, and then I slid down myself. But first I left the sign of the four upon the table. That was to show that the jewels had come back at last to those who had most right to them. Tonga pulled up the rope, closed the window, and made off the way he had come.

"I don't know that I have anything else to tell you. I had heard a water man speak of the speed of Smith's boat, the *Aurora*. So I thought she'd be handy for our escape. I hired Smith and promised him a big sum to get us safe to our ship. He knew something was wrong, but he didn't ask any questions. All this is truth. I believe my best defense is to hold back nothing. I want the world to know how badly I have been served by Major Sholto and that I am innocent of the death of his son."

"A very remarkable account," said Sherlock Holmes. "A fitting windup to an extremely interesting case. There is nothing at all new in what you say, except that you brought your own rope. That I did not know. By the way, I had hoped that Tonga had lost all his darts, yet he managed to shoot one at us in the boat."

"He had lost them all, sir," said Small. "Except the one which was in his blowpipe at the time."

"Ah, of course," said Sherlock Holmes. "I had not thought of that."

"Well, Holmes," said Athelney Jones. "I have let you and your friend do what you asked. But I shall feel safer when this fellow is under lock and key. The cab still waits and there are two inspectors downstairs. I am much obliged to you for your assistance. Of course you will be wanted at the trial. Goodnight to you."

"Goodnight, gentlemen," said Jonathan Small.

"Well, there is the end of our little drama," I remarked after a while. "I fear that it may be our last investigation together. Miss Morstan has agreed to be my wife."

"I feared as much," said Holmes. "I really cannot congratulate you."

I was a little hurt. "Have you reason to be dissatisfied with my choice?" I asked.

"Not at all. I think she is one of the most charming young ladies I have ever met. She might even have been useful in detective work. She has a certain genius that way—look at the way she saved the Agra plan from all of her father's papers. But love is an emotional thing. And emotion is opposed to reason—which you know I put above all else. No, I shall never marry.

"One last thing about this case, Watson. You see, Small did have someone working for him in the house. It could be none other than Lal Rao, the butler. So Jones actually did catch somebody on his own!"

"It seems rather unfair," I remarked. "You have done all the work in this business. I get a wife out of it and Jones gets the credit."

"I got something out of it, too," he replied. "Brain work. Now I must wait for my next case. As you know, my dear Watson, Mr. Sherlock Holmes is only happy when he is on the trail of some new adventure."

The Adventure of the Blue Carbuncle

This was the first of a second series of "adventures." In it we meet Peterson, the commissionaire. Although the word sounds like "commissioner," it is quite a different thing altogether. A Corps of Commissionaires was founded in England in 1859 to employ retired soldiers and sailors. It is true that they wore a uniform like that of a police officer, but their duties were far more modest—running errands, delivering messages, standing guard, even tending babies!

At the end of the story Holmes does a peculiar thing. He takes the law into his own hands and lets the criminal go. Holmes is famous for doing this. As an "unofficial" detective he was not obliged to turn the villain over to the police. In fact, out of sixty cases, Holmes let fourteen criminals go free.

The Adventure of the Blue Carbuncle

I called upon my good friend, Mr. Sherlock Holmes on the second morning after Christmas. I wanted to wish him the compliments of the season. I found Holmes lounging on the sofa. A huge pile of newspapers lay beside him. Next to the couch was a wooden chair. On its back hung a rather worn black felt hat and on its seat was a large magnifying glass...a tool which suggested Sherlock had been closely examining the hat.

"You are engaged," I said. "Perhaps I interrupt you..."

"Not at all! I am glad to have a friend with whom I can discuss my results. The matter is a small one," Sherlock said, pointing to the hat. "But it is interesting in its own way."

I seated myself in his armchair and warmed my hands before his crackling fire. Outside a sharp frost had set in and the windows were thick with icicles.

"I suppose," I remarked, "this hat has some deadly story linked to it. Is it the one clue that will guide you to solve some mystery and punish some criminal?"

"No, no! No crime," answered Sherlock Holmes, laughing. "Do you know Peterson, the commissionaire?"

"Yes," I replied.

"He found this hat. Its owner is unknown. It arrived on Christmas morning in the company of a good fat goose—which is now roasting in front of Peterson's fire. The facts are these: About four o'clock on Christmas morning, Peterson was walking home. The street was well-lit by a nearby gaslight. A tallish man was walking in front of him. He carried a white goose over his shoulder. At the corner stood a small gang of young ruffians. As the stranger approached, they began to bother him. One knocked off his hat. In defense, the stranger swung his walking stick over his head. The stick accidentally broke a shop window behind him. Peterson rushed forward to protect the stranger, but the man was shocked at having broken the window. On seeing an official-looking person rush toward him, he dropped his goose and took to his heels. The gang also fled. Peterson was left with this battered hat and a beautiful Christmas goose."

"Why didn't he return them to their rightful owner?" I asked.

"My dear fellow, there lies the problem. A small card was attached to the bird's left leg. On it was printed: FOR MRS. HENRY BAKER. The initials H. B. are written on the lining of the hat. But there are thousands of Bakers and hundreds of Henry Bakers in London. It is not easy to return property to any one of them."

"What did Peterson do?"

"He brought the hat and the goose to me. He knew such problems are of interest to me. We kept the goose till this morning when we realized, despite the slight frost, it should be eaten without unnecessary delay. Its finder took it home while I have the hat of the unknown gentleman who lost his Christmas dinner."

"Did he not advertise?"

"No."

"Then what clues could you have to his identity?"

"Only as much as we can deduce," answered Holmes.

"From his hat?" I asked.

"Precisely."

"But you are surely joking. What can you gather from this old battered felt hat?"

"Here is my lens." Sherlock said as he handed me his magnifying glass. "You know my methods. What can you learn from this hat about its owner?"

I took the tattered hat in my hands and turned it over. It was a very ordinary round felt hat—very much the worse for wear. There was no maker's name. However, the initials H. B. were written on one side. It was cracked, exceedingly dusty, and spotted in several places. Ink had been smeared on some of the spots to hide them.

"I can see nothing out of the ordinary," I said and handed Sherlock back the hat.

"On the contrary, Watson. You can see everything. However, you fail to reason from what you see."

"Then tell me what you can find out from this hat," I responded.

Sherlock Holmes picked up the hat and gazed at it intensely. "The owner was highly intelligent. He was fairly well-to-do within the last three years and has fallen on bad times. However he has not lost his self-respect. These are the most obvious facts that can be deduced from his hat."

"You are certainly joking, Holmes!" I exclaimed.

"Not in the least. Can it be that even after I have given you these facts you cannot see how I deduced them?"

"I must confess I cannot follow you. For example, how did you deduce that this man was intelligent?"

Holmes placed the hat on his head. It came right down over his forehead and settled on the bridge of his nose.

"It is a question of cubic capacity," he said. "A man with so large a brain must have something in it."

"The decline of his fortune then?" I asked.

"This hat is three years old. These flat brims were popular then. It is a hat of the very best quality. Look at the band of ribbed silk and the excellent lining. This man could afford to buy an expensive hat three years ago. However he has had no new hat since. His fortunes have assuredly gone down. But, he has tried to conceal some of the stains with ink. He has certainly not lost his pride."

"Your deductions are remarkable," I said. "But you said no crime has been committed and no harm done. It seems a waste of your energy."

Sherlock had just opened his mouth to answer, when the door was flung open. Peterson, the commissionaire, rushed into the room. His cheeks were flushed and he seemed dazed.

"The goose, Mr. Holmes! The goose, sir!" he gasped.

"What of it?" Sherlock asked. "Has it returned to life and flapped off through the kitchen window?"

"See here, sir! See what my wife found in its belly."

He held out an open hand. A small but brilliant blue stone dazzled in its palm.

Sherlock Holmes sat up with a whistle. "By Jove, Peterson!" he exclaimed. "This is a treasure! Do you know what you have there?"

"A diamond, sir! A precious stone! It cuts into glass as though through putty."

"It's more than a precious stone. It is *the* precious stone!"

"Not the Countess of Morcar's blue carbuncle?" I exclaimed.

"Precisely so. I ought to know its size and shape," said Holmes. "I have read about it every day in the *Times*. The stone is absolutely unique. Its value can only be guessed at. The reward of one thousand pounds is certainly not a twentieth its market price."

"A thousand pounds! Great Lord of mercy!" gasped the commissionaire. He plumped himself down into a chair and stared at us in disbelief.

"It was lost, if I remember correctly, at the Hotel Cosmopolitan," I said.

"On the twenty-second of December, just five days ago," said Holmes. "John Horner, a plumber, was charged with stealing it from the Countess' jewel case." Holmes began to rummage through his pile of newspapers. At last he found the page he was looking for. He smoothed it out, doubled it over, and read the following paragraph:

HOTEL COSMOPOLITAN JEWEL ROBBERY
JOHN HORNER, 26, PLUMBER, WAS

CHARGED WITH THE ROBBERY OF THE
COUNTESS OF MORCAR'S VALUABLE GEM
KNOWN AS THE BLUE CARBUNCLE. THE
HOTEL MANAGER, MR. JAMES RYDER,
STATED THAT HE HAD TAKEN HORNER UP
TO THE COUNTESS' ROOM TO MEND THE
BATHROOM GRATE. HE REMAINED WITH
HORNER FOR SOME TIME, BUT WAS FINAL-
LY CALLED AWAY. ON RETURNING, HE
FOUND THAT HORNER HAD DISAP-
PEARED. THE BUREAU HAD BEEN FORCED
OPEN AND THE JEWEL CASE LAY EMPTY
ON THE DRESSING TABLE. RYDER IN-
STANTLY GAVE THE ALARM. THE COUNT-
ESS' MAID, MISS CATHERINE CUSACK,
HEARD RYDER'S CRY. SHE RUSHED INTO
THE ROOM AND FOUND MATTERS EXACT-
LY AS DESCRIBED BY THE HOTEL MANA-
GER. HORNER WAS FOUND THAT SAME
EVENING. THE STONE WAS NEITHER ON
HIS PERSON NOR IN HIS ROOMS. SINCE HE
HAD BEEN CONVICTED OF A SIMILAR
CRIME ONCE BEFORE, HE WAS ARRESTED.
PROCEEDINGS WERE STARTED AGAINST
HIM IMMEDIATELY. THE ACCUSED MAN
PROTESTED HIS INNOCENCE.

"Hum!" said Holmes. "We must now figure out the
sequence of events that lead a precious stone from a
countess' jewel case to the belly of a Christmas goose!
You see, Watson, our little deductions suddenly take on

meaning. Here is the stone. The stone came from the goose . . . and the goose came from Mr. Henry Baker. We must now find him and learn what part he played in this mystery. To do this, we must try the simplest means first . . . an advertisement in the evening newspapers. If this fails, I shall have to resort to other methods."

"What will you say?" I asked.

"Give me a pencil and that slip of paper. Now then:

FOUND: A GOOSE AND A BLACK FELT HAT. MR. HENRY BAKER CAN HAVE THE SAME BY APPLYING AT 6:30 THIS EVENING AT 221B BAKER STREET.

"I believe that will do. Peterson, please run down to the advertising agency and have this printed in the evening papers. I shall keep the stone here and shall drop the Countess a note telling her that we have found it. On your way back buy a goose. We must have one to give to Mr. Baker in place of the one your family is devouring right now!"

That evening at half-past six I returned to Baker Street. Holmes and I had agreed to have dinner together after our visitor left. As I approached the house I saw a tall man waiting outside. Just as I arrived the door was opened. We were both shown up to Sherlock Holmes' rooms.

"Ah, Watson, you have come at the right time," said Holmes. He turned to the tall man, "Mr. Henry Baker, I believe. Pray take this chair by the fire." He handed the man the hat and added, "Is this your hat, Mr. Baker?"

"Yes, sir," replied Baker. He was a large man with rounded shoulders, a massive head, and a broad, intelligent face. His black frock coat was buttoned high in front with the collar turned up. There was no sign of either cuff or shirt beneath.

"Why didn't you advertise your loss?" Holmes asked.

Our visitor gave a rather shame-faced laugh. "Shillings have not been as plentiful with me as they once were," he remarked. "I assumed the gang of ruffians carried off both my hat and the bird. I did not care to spend money in a hopeless attempt to recover them."

"Naturally. By the way, about the bird—we were compelled to eat it."

"To eat it!" exclaimed our visitor. He half rose from his chair in agitation.

"Yes, it would have been no use to anyone had we not done so. But I presume this other goose on the sideboard will do. It is about the same weight and perfectly fresh."

"Oh, certainly, certainly!" answered Mr. Baker with a sigh of relief.

"Of course, we still have the feathers, legs, belly and so on of your own bird. So if you wish..."

"They might be useful to me as relics of my adventure," said Baker, "but beyond that I can hardly see what use they would be."

Sherlock glanced sharply across at me. He shrugged his shoulders.

"There is your hat and there is your bird. By the way," Sherlock said, "would it bore you to tell me where you got the other one from? I am somewhat of a fowl fancier and I have seldom seen a better-grown goose."

"Certainly, sir. A number of my friends and I often visit the Alpha Inn near the museum. This year our good host, Mr. Windigate, started a goose club. We were to pay a few pennies each week and in exchange receive a goose at Christmas. I paid my weekly pennies and was taking home the bird the other night. You know what followed." Mr. Henry Baker took up his bird and hat, thanked us, and departed.

"So much for Mr. Henry Baker," said Holmes. "It is quite certain that he knows nothing about the matter. Shall we turn our dinner into a late supper and follow up our clue while it is hot?"

"By all means!" I agreed enthusiastically.

We bundled up and went outdoors. It was a bitter night and the breath of passersby hung in the air like smoke. Our footsteps rang out crisply as we walked. In a quarter of an hour we were at the Alpha Inn. Holmes immediately ordered two glasses of beer from the ruddy-faced landlord.

"Your beer should be excellent if it is as good as your geese!" Holmes told the landlord.

"My geese!" exclaimed the landord, Windigate.

"Yes. I was speaking only half an hour ago to Mr. Henry Baker. He is a member of your goose club."

"Ah yes, I see. But they weren't my geese."

"Indeed!" said Holmes. "Whose then?"

"Well, I got the two dozen from a salesman in Covent Garden Market."

"I know some of them!" exclaimed Holmes. "Which salesman was it?"

"Breckinridge is his name."

"Ah! I don't know him. Well, here's to your good health and to the prosperity of your inn." Sherlock drank his beer, rose from his seat, and motioned for me to follow. In a moment we were standing outside once again.

"Now for Mr. Breckinridge," Holmes said. "Remember, Watson, a man may get seven years imprisonment if we cannot prove his innocence. Our only clue is a Christmas goose that somehow had a gem in its belly. Our inquiry may lead to Horner's guilt, but we must follow it through to the bitter end."

By the time we reached Covent Garden Market it was near closing time. There were still many people milling about. One of the largest stalls bore the name of Breckinridge. Beneath the sign stood the man himself. He had a rather sharp face and trim side-whiskers and was helping a boy shut up the shutters.

"Sold out of geese, I see," Holmes commented, pointing at the bare slabs of marble.

"Let you have five hundred tomorrow morning," muttered Breckinridge.

"That's no good," Holmes answered.

"Well, there are still some at the next stall," replied the salesman.

"Ah, but I was recommended to you."

"Who by?" he asked.

"The landlord of the Alpha."

"Ah yes, I sent him a couple of dozen," Breckinridge answered.

"Fine birds they were too," Holmes replied. "Where did you get them from?"

To my surprise the question provoked a burst of anger from the salesman.

"What are you driving at?" he asked. "Let's have it straight now."

"It is straight enough," said Sherlock. "I should like to know who sold you the geese which you then sold to Alpha."

"Well, I shan't tell you!" responded Breckinridge.

"Oh! It is a matter of no importance. But I don't know why you should be so hot over such a small thing."

"Hot! You'd be hot, if you were as pestered as I am. When I pay good money for a good article that should be an end to the business. But it's 'Where are the geese?' and 'What will you take for the geese?' and 'Who did you sell the geese to?' One would think they were the only geese in the world to hear the fuss that is made over them."

"Well, I have no connection with any other people," Holmes said carelessly. "But I bet five pounds that the bird I ate was country bred."

"Well then, you've lost your money. It was town bred," snapped the salesman.

"It was nothing of the kind!" insisted Sherlock.

"I say it was!"

"I don't believe it."

"Do you think you know more about birds than I do?" asked Breckinridge. "I've been handling them since I was a child. I tell you all the birds that went to the Alpha were town bred."

"Will you bet then?" prodded Holmes.

"It's merely taking your money, for I know I am right. But I'll bet just to teach you not to be so stubborn."

The salesman chuckled grimly. "Bring me my books, Bill," he ordered.

The boy brought back a small ledger and a large greasy one. He placed them both on a slab of marble beneath a hanging lamp.

"You see this little book," said Breckinridge. "It contains a list of the people from whom I buy. Here on this page are the country folk and the numbers after their names are where their accounts are in the big ledger. You see this other page in red ink? Well, this is a list of my town suppliers. Now, look at the third name. Just read it out to me."

"Mrs. Oakshott, 117 Brixton Road—page 249," read Holmes.

"Quite so. Now turn to page 249 in the large ledger."

Holmes turned to that page. On it was written: "Mrs. Oakshott, 117 Brixton Road, egg and poultry supplier."

"Now what is the last entry?" asked the salesman.

"December 22, 24 geese."

"Quite so. There you are . . . and underneath?"

"Sold to Mr. Windigate of the Alpha."

"What have you to say now?" asked Breckinridge triumphantly.

Sherlock looked deeply upset. He drew a coin out of his pocket and threw it down onto the slab. Then he turned away in disgust. A few yards off he stopped under a lamppost and laughed in a hearty, noiseless fashion. "Well, Watson," he said to me. "I fancy we are nearing the end of our quest. The only question that remains is whether we should go on to this Mrs. Oakshott's tonight or tomorrow. It is clear there are others who are anxious about the matter, and I should. . ."

Just then a commotion broke out at the stall we had just left.

"I've had enough of you and your geese!" Mr. Breckinridge was shouting at a little cringing man. "If you come pestering me anymore with your silly talk I'll set the dog on you. You bring Mrs. Oakshott here and I'll answer her, but what have you to do with it? Did I buy the geese off you?"

"No, but one of them was mine just the same," whined the little man.

"Well, then ask Mrs. Oakshott for it!"

"She told me to ask you."

"You can ask the King of Prussia for all I care! I've had enough. Get out!!!" He rushed fiercely forward. The little man ran quickly into the darkness.

"Ha, this may save us a visit to Brixton Road," whispered Holmes. My companion speedily overtook the man and touched him on the shoulder. The man sprang around nervously. I could see by the gaslight that his face was deathly pale.

"Who are you? What do you want?" he asked in a shaken voice.

"My name is Sherlock Holmes. It is my business to know what other people don't know."

"But you know nothing of this," the man insisted.

"Excuse me, I know everything of it," Holmes replied. "You are trying to trace some geese. They were sold by Mrs. Oakshott of Brixton Road to a salesman named Breckinridge. They were in turn sold to Mr. Windigate of the Alpha and by him to Mr. Henry Baker."

"Oh sir, you are the very man whom I have longed to meet," cried the little fellow.

Sherlock Holmes hailed a cab. "In that case we had better discuss the matter in the privacy of my rooms. Who do I have the pleasure of assisting?"

"My name is John Robinson," he answered.

"No, no. The real name," said Holmes, sweetly. "It is always awkward doing business with an alias."

The stranger's cheeks turned red, "Well, then," he said, "my real name is James Ryder."

"Precisely so! Manager of the Hotel Cosmopolitan! Step into the cab and I shall be able to tell you everything you wish to know presently." Holmes motioned toward the waiting cab.

The little man stood glancing from one of us to the other. His eyes were half frightened and half hopeful. Then he stepped into the cab. In half an hour we were back at Baker Street. Nothing had been said during the drive. But our companion's heavy breathing told us how nervous he was.

"Here we are!" said Sherlock cheerfully as we filed into the room. "The fire looks very seasonable in this weather. You look cold, Mr. Ryder. Take this basket-chair. I will just put on my slippers before we settle this little matter of yours. Now then! You want to know what became of those geese? Or rather, of that goose. It was one bird, I imagine, which interests you—white with a black bar across its tail."

Ryder quivered with emotion. "Oh, sir," he cried, "can you tell me where it went?"

"It came here."

"Here?"

"Yes and a most remarkable bird it proved to be. I don't wonder that you should take an interest in it. It laid an egg after it was dead—the brightest little blue egg that ever was seen. I have it right here."

Our visitor staggered to his feet and steadied himself against the mantelpiece. Holmes unlocked his strong box and held up the blue carbuncle. It shone out like a star. Ryder glanced at it, uncertain whether to claim it or disown it.

"The game's up, Ryder," Holmes said quietly. Ryder staggered, nearly falling into the fire. I helped him into his chair and gave him a dash of brandy. He sat staring at his accuser.

"I have deduced most of the facts of this case. There is little for you to tell me," said Holmes. "Still, that little may as well be cleared up. How did you first learn of the Countess' stone?"

"It was Catherine Cusack who told me of it," he said.

"I see. Her ladyship's maid. And the temptation of easy wealth was too much for you. You knew the plumber Horner had once been involved in a similar matter. He would immediately be suspected. So what did you do? You created a job for him in the Countess' room. When he was done, you stole the gem, raised the alarm and had him arrested. You then . . ."

Ryder threw himself on the rug. "For God's sake, have mercy," he shrieked. "Think of my father! Of my mother! It would break their hearts. I never went wrong before! I never will again. I swear it. I'll swear it on a Bible. Oh don't bring it into court!"

"Get back into your chair!" said Holmes sternly. "It

is all very well for you to cringe and crawl now. You thought little of poor Horner in prison for your crime."

"I will flee, Mr. Holmes. I will leave the country. Then the charge against him will be dropped."

"Hum! We will talk about that later. And now let us hear the true account of the next act. How did the stone come to be in the goose and the goose come to be in the market? Your safety depends on you telling us the truth."

Ryder passed his tongue over his parched lips. "I will tell you just as it happened, sir," he said. "I had to hide the stone. There was no safe hiding place in the hotel. After Horner was arrested, I went to my sister's house. She is married to a man named Oakshott. She lives on Brixton Road and breeds birds in her backyard. Along the way I suspected each man I saw of being a policeman or detective. By the time I got to Brixton Road sweat was pouring down my face. My sister asked me what was the matter. I told her the jewel robbery at the hotel had upset me. Then I went into the back yard, smoked a pipe and wondered what to do next.

"I remembered a friend called Maudsley. He knew the ways of thieves and how they got rid of what they stole. I made up my mind to go to Kilburn where he lived. He would show me how to turn the stone into money. But how to get it to him? . . . At any moment I could be seized and searched. And there was the stone in my pocket. I looked down at the geese waddling about me feet. Suddenly an idea came into my head—one which would stump the best detective that ever lived!

"My sister had promised me a goose for Christmas. I would take my goose now and in it I would carry my stone to Kilburn. I spotted a fine white bird with a distinctive tail. I caught the bird and pried open its bill. Then I thrust the stone down its throat. The bird gave a gulp. I felt the stone pass along its gullet and into its belly. The bird flapped and struggled. Out came my sister. As I turned to speak to her, the bird broke loose and joined the others.

" 'Whatever were you doing with that bird, Jim?' she asked.

" 'Well, you said you'd give me one for Christmas. I was feeling to see which one was the fattest.'

" 'Oh! We've set yours aside for you. Jim's bird, we call it. It's the big, white one over yonder. There's twenty-six of them, which makes one for you and one for us and two dozen for the market.'

" 'Thank you, Maggie,' says I. 'But if it is all the same to you, I'd rather have that one I was handling just now.'

" 'The other is a good three pounds heavier,' she said. 'We fattened it expressly for you.'

" 'Never mind, I'll have the other and I'll take it now.'

" 'Oh, very well,' she answered. 'Kill it and take it with you.'

"Well, I did what she said, Mr. Holmes, and I carried the bird all the way to Kilburn. I told my pal what I had done and he laughed until he nearly choked. We got a knife and opened the goose. But there was no stone. I immediately knew there had been some terrible mistake. I left the bird and rushed back to my sister's. But there was not one bird to be seen.

" 'Where are they all, Maggie?' I cried.

" 'Gone to the dealer's, Jim.'

" 'Which dealer's?'

" 'Breckinridge of Covent Garden.'

" 'But was there another with a barred tail?' I asked. 'The same as the one I chose?'

" 'Yes, Jim,' she answered. 'There were two barred-tailed ones. I could never tell them apart.'

"Well, then I realized what had happened. I ran off as fast as my feet would carry me to Breckinridge. He had sold them and wouldn't tell me where they had gone. You heard him yourselves. My sister thinks I am going mad. Sometimes I think I am, too! And now—and now I am myself a branded thief. Without ever having touched the wealth for which I sold my character! God help me!" He burst into sobs and buried his face in his hands.

There was a long silence broken only by Ryder's sobs and Sherlock's fingers tapping on the table beside him. Finally my friend rose and threw open the door.

"Get out!" he told the man.

"What, sir?" Ryder exclaimed in disbelief. "Oh, heaven bless you!"

"No more words. Get out!"

And no more words were needed. There was a sudden rush to the door, a clatter on the stairs, the bang of the front door, and the rattle of running footsteps from the street.

"After all, Watson," said Holmes, reaching for his clay pipe, "I am not employed by the police. If Horner were in danger it would be another thing. But this fellow will not testify against him. The case will collapse. I suppose I should turn him in. But perhaps by setting him free I am saving his soul. This fellow will not go wrong again. He is too frightened. Send him to jail now and you make him a jailbird for life. Besides, it is the season of forgiveness. Chance put a curious mystery in our hands. Our solution is our reward.

"And now, Dr. Watson. Please ring Mrs. Hudson, the housekeeper . . . It is time to investigate yet another bird—one which she has kindly prepared for our supper."

The Adventure of the Speckled Band

Of all the Sherlock Holmes stories, this was Conan Doyle's favorite. He ranked it number one on a list of the twelve stories he liked best. He was not alone in his choice. In 1927 readers of the British newspaper *The Observer* were asked to pick their twelve favorites. They, too, ranked *The Adventure of the Speckled Band* as number one.

Conan Doyle wrote a play version of this adventure in just two weeks. It opened in London on June 4, 1910. The play was a huge success and ran for 169 continuous performances. *The Adventure of the Speckled Band* was so popular in fact that it was chosen as the subject of a movie. In 1931 the film *The Speckled Band* opened to enthusiastic audiences both in England and America. The well-known actor Raymond Massey played Sherlock Holmes.

The Adventure of
the Speckled Band

The strange adventure of the speckled band occurred when I was still a bachelor, sharing rooms with my friend, Mr. Sherlock Holmes. It is the most fantastic of all the cases I have written.

It all began in April of 1883. I woke one morning to find Sherlock Holmes standing fully dressed by my bed. I blinked up at him in surprise. The clock on the mantelpiece showed that it was only a quarter past seven.

"Very sorry to wake you, Watson," he said.

"What is it then," I asked. "A fire?"

"No, a client. It seems a young lady has arrived and is quite upset. She insists on seeing me. She is waiting in the sitting room now. When young ladies wander about the city at this hour, and wake sleepy people from their beds, it is usually for some urgent reason. I know you like to follow interesting cases from the beginning. So I thought I should wake you and give you that chance."

"My dear fellow," I said, excitedly. "I would not miss it for anything." There was nothing I enjoyed more than observing Holmes during an investigation. I greatly admired his rapid deductions which were swift as intuition, but always based on logic. I quickly threw on my clothes. A few minutes later Holmes and I walked into the sitting room. A darkly dressed lady rose as we entered the room. She wore a heavy veil.

"Good morning, madam," Holmes said cheerfully. "My name is Sherlock Holmes. This is my intimate friend and associate, Dr. Watson. You can speak freely in front of him. Ha, I see that our housekeeper, Mrs. Hudson, has lighted a fire. Please draw your chair up to it. I shall order you a cup of hot coffee, for I observe that you are shivering."

"It is not the cold that makes me shiver," she said in a low voice.

"What then?" asked Holmes.

"It is fear, Mr. Holmes. It is terror!" She raised her veil as she spoke. Her face was drawn and gray and her eyes were frightened and restless like those of a hunted animal. Her features and figure were young, but her hair was streaked with gray.

"You must not fear," Sherlock said soothingly. "We shall soon set matters right. You have come by train, I see."

"You know me then?" she asked nervously.

"No, but I observe the second half of a return ticket in the palm of your left glove. You must have started early and yet you had a long drive in a carriage before you reached the train station."

The lady gave a violent start and stared at my friend in confusion.

"There is no mystery, my dear madam," said he, smiling. "The left arm of your jacket is spattered with mud in at least seven places. The marks are fresh. An open carriage is the only vehicle that throws up mud in that way."

"You are perfectly correct," she said. "I started from home before six, reached the train depot at twenty past, and came by the first train. Sir, I can stand this strain no longer. I shall go mad if it continues. I have no one to turn to. There is one man who cares for me, but he can be of little help. Oh, sir, do you think that you can help me? At present I can't reward you for your services, but in a month or six weeks I shall be married and in control of my own money. At that time, you will not find me ungrateful."

"My profession is its own reward," said Holmes. "But you can pay for my expenses. Now please tell us what is troubling you."

"My name is Helen Stoner. I live with my stepfather, who is the last survivor of one of the oldest Saxon families in England—the Roylotts of Stoke Moran.

"The family was once among the richest in England. Over the years the riches were spent foolishly. Eventually nothing was left but a few acres of land and a two-hundred-year-old house with a heavy mortgage. The last squire lived there as a pauper. His son—my stepfather—realized that he must do something to help himself. He borrowed money from a relative and studied medicine. Then he went to India where he set up a large practice. There were a series of robberies involving his native butler. In a fit of anger he beat the butler to death. He was arrested and remained in prison a long time. He returned to England a disappointed and bitter man.

"When Dr. Roylott was in India he married my mother, Mrs. Stoner. She was a widow with twin daughters, Julia and myself. We were only two years old at the time of their remarriage. She had a small fortune which she turned over to Dr. Roylott. There was one provision, however. We were to be given a yearly sum should we marry. Shortly after our return to England, my mother died. She was killed eight years ago in a railway accident. Dr. Roylott gave up efforts to start a medical practice in London and took us to live with him in the old house in Surrey. The money my mother had left was enough for all our wants. There now seemed to be no obstacle to our happiness.

"But a terrible change came over my stepfather at that time. He shut himself up in the house and quarreled with anyone who crossed his path. His temper was so violent and his strength so immense that people would flee when he approached.

"Last week he hurled the local blacksmith into a stream. It was only by paying him off that I stopped a public scandal. He has no friends except the wandering gypsies. He lets them camp out on the land and sometimes wanders away with them for weeks. He has a passion for Indian animals. At this moment a cheetah and a baboon wander freely over the grounds. They are feared by the villagers as much as their master.

"My sister Julia and I had little pleasure in our lives. No servant would stay with us. For a long time we did all the housework ourselves. Julia was only thirty when she died, but her hair had already begun to whiten, as has mine."

"Your sister is dead, then?"

"She died two years ago. It is of her death that I wish to speak to you. As you can imagine, we had little opportunity to meet anyone our own age. We had, however, an aunt—our mother's sister, who lived nearby. Occasionally, we were allowed to pay her short visits. Julia went there at Christmas two years ago. She met a major to whom she became engaged. My stepfather learned of the engagement and did not object. But within two weeks a terrible event happened which took away my only companion."

Sherlock Holmes had been leaning back in his chair with his eyes closed. He now half-opened them and glanced at his visitor.

"Please be precise with the details," he said.

"It is easy for me to be so. Every event of that dreadful time is seared into my memory. As I have already said, the manor house is very old. Only one wing is now lived in. The bedrooms in this wing are on the ground floor. The first is Dr. Roylott's, the second is my sister's and the third is mine. They all open out onto the same corridor. Do I make myself clear?"

"Precisely so."

"The windows of the three rooms open out onto the lawn. That fatal night, Dr. Roylott had gone to his room early. We knew that he had not gone to sleep as my sister was bothered by the smell of the strong Indian cigars he smokes. She left her room because of it, and came to mine. She remained for some time, chatting about her approaching wedding. At eleven o'clock she rose to leave, but paused at the door.

" 'Tell me, Helen,' she said. 'Have you ever heard anyone whistle in the dead of night?'

" 'Never,' said I.

" 'I suppose that you couldn't whistle in your sleep?'

" 'Certainly not. But why?'

" 'Because during the last few nights at about three

in the morning I have heard a low, clear whistle. I am a light sleeper and it has awakened me. I cannot tell where it comes from, perhaps from the next room, perhaps from the lawn. Have you heard it?'

" 'No, I have not,' I said. 'It must be those wretched gypsies.'

" 'Very likely. And yet you would have heard it had it come from the lawn.'

" 'Ah, but I sleep more heavily than you.'

" 'Well, it isn't important,' she said. She smiled back at me, closed my door, and a few minutes later I heard her key turn in the lock."

"Indeed," said Holmes. "Do you always lock yourselves in at night?"

"Always"

"And why?"

"I think I mentioned to you that the Doctor kept a cheetah and a baboon. We felt more secure with the doors locked."

"Quite so. Proceed with your statement."

"I could not sleep that night. I felt uneasy. It was a wild night. The wind was howling outside. The rain was beating and splashing against the windows. Suddenly, I heard the wild scream of a terrified woman. I knew it was my sister's voice. I sprang from my bed, wrapped a shawl around me, and rushed into the corridor. As I opened my door I heard a low whistle. It was soon followed by a clanging sound, as if something metal had fallen. As I ran toward my sister's door, it slowly opened. I stared at it, horror stricken, not knowing what would come forth. By the light of the hall lamp I saw my sister standing in the doorway. Her face was white with terror, her hands groped for help, she swayed back and forth. I ran to her and threw my arms around her. But at that moment her legs gave way. She fell to the ground. She writhed as though in terrible pain. At first I thought that she hadn't recognized me. But as I bent over her she suddenly shrieked, 'Oh my God! Helen! It was the band. The speckled band!' She was about to speak again and pointed to the Doctor's room, but a fresh wave of pain seized her. I called loudly for my stepfather. He rushed from his room in his dressing gown. When he reached my sister's side she was unconscious. He poured brandy down her throat and sent for medical aid from the village. But it was no use. She died without regaining consciousness. Such was the dreadful end of my beloved sister."

"One moment," said Holmes. "Are you sure about this whistle and the metallic sound? Could you swear to it?"

"It is my strong impression that I heard it. But with the crash of the winds outside and the creaking of an old house, it is possible I was mistaken."

"Was your sister dressed?" Holmes asked.

"No, she was in her nightdress. In her right hand was a charred matchstick and in her left hand was a matchbox."

"Showing that she had struck a light and looked around her. That is important. And what conclusions did the coroner come to?"

"He investigated the case with great care. He did not find any satisfactory cause of death. The door had been closed from within. The windows were barred by shutters with iron bars which were locked each night.

The walls of her room were solid as was the floor. It is certain therefore that my sister was quite alone. Besides, there were no marks of violence upon her."

"How about poison?"

"The doctors found none."

"What do you think she died of?" Sherlock asked.

"It is my belief that she died of pure fear and nervous shock. But I can't imagine what frightened her so," Miss Stoner answered.

"Were the gypsies on the land at the time?"

"Yes, there are nearly always some there."

"Ah, and what do you think she meant by 'speckled band'?"

"Sometimes I think it was merely the wild talk of fear. Other times I think it referred to some band of people . . . perhaps to the gypsies—perhaps to the spotted handkerchiefs so many wear around their heads."

Holmes shook his head. He looked far from satisfied.

"Two years have passed since then," continued the lady. "Until recently my life was lonelier than ever. But a month ago a dear friend asked my hand in marriage. My stepfather did not oppose the match. We are to be married in the spring. Two days ago some repairs were started on the house. A hole was made in my bedroom wall. I have had to move to the room where my sister died. I have had to sleep in the very bed where she slept. Imagine my terror last night when I heard the same whistle that she had heard before she died. I jumped out of bed and lit the lamp, but there was nothing to see. I was too shaken to go to bed again. So I dressed and as soon as it was daylight, I slipped out of the house and made my way to you."

"You have done wisely," said my friend. "But have you told me all?"

"Yes, all."

"Miss Stoner, you have not. You are screening your stepfather."

"Why? What do you mean?" she asked.

Holmes pushed back the frill of lace that decorated her sleeve. Five little bruises—the marks of four fingers and a thumb—were printed on her white wrist.

"You have been cruelly treated," said Sherlock Holmes.

The lady blushed and covered up her injured wrist. "He is a hard man," she said, "and perhaps he does not know his own strength."

Holmes leaned his chin on his hands and stared silently into the fire for some minutes.

"This is serious business," he said at last. "There are a thousand details I must know before I decide what to do. But we haven't a moment to lose. If we come to Stoke Moran today can we look over the bedrooms without your stepfather knowing?"

"He spoke of coming into town today on important business. He will probably be away all day. We have a housekeeper, but she is old and foolish. I can easily keep her out of the way."

"Excellent. Will you join me, Watson?"

"By all means," I answered at once.

"Then we shall both come. What are you going to do, Miss Stoner?"

"I have one or two things to do in town. But I shall return by the twelve o'clock train. I will be there in time for your arrival."

"You may expect us early in the afternoon," said Holmes. "I have myself some small business matters to attend to. Will you join us for breakfast?"

"No, I must go. My heart is lighter now that I have confided in you. I shall look forward to seeing you again this afternoon." She dropped her thick veil back over her face and glided from the room.

"And what do you think of it all, Watson?" Sherlock asked me after she had left.

"It seems to me to be a most dark and sinister business," I said.

"Yes, both dark and sinister," agreed Sherlock.

"If the walls and floors are solid and the windows were barred and the door was locked, then her sister must have been alone when she met her mysterious end."

"What about the nightly whistles and the very peculiar words of the dying woman?" added Sherlock.

"I cannot think."

"When you combine whistles at night with the presence of a band of gypsies, a stepfather who has much to lose by his stepdaughter's marriage, her strange dying words, and the metallic clang her sister heard, it does seem to point to the gypsies."

"But what did the gypsies do?" I asked.

"I cannot imagine," Holmes answered seriously.

"I see many objections to such a theory."

"And so do I. It is precisely for that reason that we are going to Stoke Moran today. But what the devil?!"

The door was flung open. A huge man now stood in the doorway. He wore a black top hat, a long frock coat, and a pair of tall boots. He held a whip in his hand. He was so tall that his hat brushed the crossbar of the doorway. He was so wide that he seemed to fill it from side to side. His face was tanned and wrinkled and his deep-set eyes and high, thin nose made him look like a fierce old bird of prey.

"Which of you is Holmes?" he demanded.

"I am," said Holmes quietly.

"I am Dr. Grimesby Roylott, of Stoke Moran."

"Indeed, Doctor," said Holmes blandly. "Please take a seat."

"I will do nothing of the kind. My stepdaughter has been here. I have traced her. What has she been saying to you?" screamed the old man furiously.

"I hear the spring flowers are blooming in the country," Sherlock commented.

"Ha! You put me off, do you?" said our new visitor. He took a step forward and shook his hunting crop. "I know you, you scoundrel. I have heard of you before. You are Holmes the meddler!"

My friend smiled.

"Holmes the busybody!"

His smile broadened.

"Holmes the snoop."

Holmes chuckled heartily, "Your conversation is most entertaining," he said. "When you go out, close the door . . . there is a draught."

"I will go when I have had my say. Don't you dare meddle in my affairs. I know Miss Stoner has been here—I traced her! I am a dangerous man to cross! See here!" He stepped forward swiftly and seized the steel firepoker and bent it into a curve with his huge brown hands.

"See that you keep yourself out of my way," he snarled and hurled the twisted poker into the fireplace. Then he strode out of the room.

"He seems a very pleasant person, no?" said Holmes, laughing. "If he had remained, I could have shown him my own strength." As he spoke he picked up the steel poker. With a sudden effort he straightened it out again.

"This incident with the Doctor adds interest to the case. But I do hope our little friend will not suffer because of her visit to us. And now, Watson, we shall order breakfast and afterward I shall take a walk."

It was nearly one o'clock when Sherlock Holmes returned from his walk. He held a sheet of blue paper in his hand. Notes and figures were scrawled on it.

"I have seen the will of the dead wife," he said. "It seems her fortune is not worth that much anymore. If both girls were married, their stepfather would be left with very little. If even one married his lifestyle would have to change drastically. My morning's work has not been wasted. It proves that he has a very strong reason for stopping his stepdaughters' marriages. We must hurry to the train. Please, slip your revolver into your pocket. A gun can be an excellent argument against a man who can twist steel pokers into knots! That and a toothbrush are all that we need."

We drove by cab to the train station and from there traveled by train to Leatherhead, the nearest train depot to Miss Stoner's home. We hired a carriage and driver to take us to the Roylott mansion in Stoke Moran. During the drive, Sherlock sat deep in thought. His arms were folded, his hat was pulled down over his eyes and his chin was sunk down upon his chest. Suddenly, however, he tapped me on the shoulder and pointed over the meadows.

"Look there!" said he.

In the distance I could see the wooded grounds and gray gables of a very old mansion.

"Stoke Moran?" he asked the driver.

"Yes, sir, that's the house of Dr. Grimesby Roylott."

"There is some building going on there," said Holmes. "That is where we are going."

"There's the village," said the driver. He pointed to a cluster of rooftops some distance to the left. "But if you want to get to the house, you'll find it shorter to get out and walk by footpath over the fields. There it is, where the lady is walking."

"And the lady, I fancy, is Miss Stoner," observed Holmes, shading his eyes. "Yes, I think we had better do what you suggest."

We got off, paid our fare, and the carriage rattled back down the road.

"I thought it best for that fellow to think we came here on business," commented Holmes. "Good afternoon, Miss Stoner."

Our client had hurried to meet us. "I have been waiting so eagerly for you," she said happily. "All has turned out splendidly. Dr. Roylott has gone to town and it is unlikely he will be back before evening."

"We have had the pleasure of making the Doctor's acquaintance," said Holmes. In a few words he sketched out what had occurred. Miss Stoner turned white to the lips.

"Good heavens!" she cried. "He followed me then."

"So it appears."

"He is so cunning. I never know when I am safe from him. What will he say when he returns?"

"He may find that someone even more cunning than he is on his track. You must lock yourself up from him tonight. If he is violent, we will take you to your aunt's tomorrow. Let us examine the bedrooms immediately."

The building was built of gray stone. There were three distinct wings to the house. The left wing had broken and boarded-up windows and the roof was caving in. The central portion was in a little better repair but obviously was not in use. The right-hand building seemed modern. There were blinds in the windows and blue smoke curled from one of the chimneys. This was where the family lived. A scaffold leaned against the end wall although there were no signs of workmen about. Holmes walked up and down the ill-trimmed lawn. He examined the outside of the windows carefully.

"I take it, this is the window to your old bedroom," he said, pointing to the farthest window. "The center one is to your sister's room and the one next to the main building is to Dr. Roylott's room. Is that right?"

"Exactly so. But I am now sleeping in the middle room," said Miss Stoner.

"Because of the repairs. By the way, there doesn't seem to be any real need for repairs to that end wall."

"No, there isn't. I believe it was an excuse to move me from my room."

"Ah! I see," said Holmes. "Would you please go into your room and bar your shutters?"

Miss Stoner did so. Holmes tried in every way to force the shutters open, but they would not budge. He tested the hinges as well, but they were solid iron and attached firmly to the stone wall. "Hum!" said he, scratching his head. "My theory presents some difficulties. No one could pass through these shutters if they were bolted. Well, let us go within and see if we learn anything there."

A small side door led to a white-washed corridor. Three bedrooms opened off it. Holmes would not examine the third room. We went immediately to the middle room where Miss Stoner now slept. It was a cosy little room with a low ceiling and a gaping fireplace. There was little furniture in the room. The floorboards were old and worn as was the wood paneling which covered the walls. Holmes drew one of the chairs into the corner and sat down. His eyes traveled around and around and up and down, taking in every detail of the room.

"To what room does that bell connect?" he asked at last. He pointed to a thick bell-rope which hung beside the bed. The tassel at its end lay upon the pillow.

"It goes to the housekeeper's room."

"It looks newer than the other objects in the room."

"Yes, it was only put there a couple of years ago," Miss Stoner answered.

"Your sister asked for it, I suppose?" asked Holmes.

"No, I never heard of her using it. We used to get what we wanted for ourselves."

"Indeed, it seemed unnecessary to put so nice a bell-pull there. You will excuse me for a few minutes while I examine this floor . . ." Sherlock Holmes lay face-down on the floor. He held his magnifying glass in his hand and crawled backward and forward, examining the cracks between the boards. Then he examined the wood paneling. He walked over to the bed. He spent some time staring at it and running his eye up and down the wall. Finally he took the bell-rope in his hand and gave it a good pull.

"Why, it's a fake," he said.

"Won't it ring?" she asked.

"No, it isn't even attached to a wire. This is very interesting. It is attached to a hook in the ventilator shaft."

"How very absurd! I never noticed that before."

"Very strange!" muttered Holmes and pulled at the rope. "There are a few curious things about this room. For example, what fool builder would put in a ventilator between two rooms when he could have connected it directly to the outside air?!"

"That is also quite new," said the lady.

"Done about the same time as the bell-rope?" asked Holmes.

"Yes, there were several little changes made at that time."

"They seem to be of a particularly odd nature—fake bell-ropes and ventilators which do not ventilate! With your permission, Miss Stoner, I would now like to examine your stepfather's room."

Dr. Grimesby Roylott's bedroom was large and

plainly furnished. There was a camp bed, a wooden shelf full of books, an armchair beside the bed, a plain wooden chair against the wall, a round table, and a large iron safe. Holmes walked slowly around the room and examined each item.

"What's in here?" he asked, tapping the safe.

"My stepfather's business papers," Miss Stoner answered.

"Oh! You have seen inside then?" asked Holmes.

"Only once, years ago. I remember it was full of papers."

"There isn't a cat in it, is there?" Holmes asked.

"No. What a strange idea."

"Well, look at this!" He picked up a small saucer of milk which was on top.

"No, we don't keep a cat. But there is a cheetah and a baboon."

"Ah, yes, of course! Well, a cheetah is just a big cat, and yet a saucer of milk seems a bit small for its great thirst. There is one more thing I want to see." He squatted down in front of the wooden chair and examined the seat of it carefully.

"Thank you. That is quite settled," said he. He rose and put his lens into his pocket. "Hullo! Here is something interesting!"

A whip hung on one corner of the bed. The end of it was knotted into a nooselike loop.

"What do you make of that, Watson?"

"It's a common enough whip," I answered. "But I don't know why it's knotted like that."

"That is not quite so common, is it? Ah, me! It is a

wicked world when a clever man turns his brains to crime. I think that I have seen enough now, Miss Stoner. With your permission we shall walk on the lawn."

I had never seen my friend's face look so grim. We walked several times up and down the lawn and neither Miss Stoner nor myself said a word. Sherlock was the first to speak. "It is very essential, Miss Stoner, that you follow my advice in every way."

"I shall most certainly do so," she said.

"Your life may depend on it!" he added.

"I will follow your directions exactly."

"In the first place, my friend and I must spend the night in your room."

Both Miss Stoner and I gazed at him in astonishment.

"Yes," he said, "it must be so. Let me explain. I believe that is the village inn over there?" He pointed to a large building in the distance.

"Yes, that is The Crown," she answered.

"Very good. Your windows can be seen from there?"

"Certainly."

"On your stepfather's return you must say that you have a headache and go to your room. When he retires for the night, you must open your shutters, put your lamp in the window as a signal to us, and then quietly go into your old room. In spite of the repairs, can you stay there for one night?"

"Oh, yes, easily."

"The rest you will leave in our hands," said Holmes.

"But what will you do?" asked Miss Stoner.

"We shall spend the night in your room, and investigate the noise which has disturbed you."

"I believe, Mr. Holmes, that you have already made up your mind as to this case," said Miss Stoner.

"Perhaps I have."

"Then for pity's sake tell me what was the cause of my sister's death."

"I should prefer to have more proof before I speak," he answered.

"You can at least tell me whether my own idea was correct. Did she die from sudden fright?"

"No, I do not think so. I think the cause of death was more definite. And now, Miss Stoner, we must leave you. If Dr. Roylott returned and saw us, everything would be ruined. Be brave. If you follow my directions, I believe we can end this nightmare."

Sherlock Holmes and I had no trouble renting a room at the local inn, The Crown. It was on the upper floor and had a view of the right wing of the manor house. At dusk, we saw Dr. Grimesby Roylott drive past. His huge form loomed above the lad who drove him. The boy had some difficulty undoing the heavy iron gates. We heard the hoarse roar of the Doctor's voice. We saw the fury with which he clenched his fists at him. The carriage drove on. A few minutes later we saw a light spring up among the trees. A lamp was lit in one of the sitting rooms.

"Do you know, Watson," said Holmes as we sat together in the darkness. "I have some hesitation about taking you with me tonight. This is a dangerous case."

"Can I be of assistance?" I asked.

"Your presence might be most necessary."

"Then I shall certainly come," I said.

"It is very kind of you," Holmes said.

"You speak of danger," I commented. "You have certainly seen more in these bedrooms than I have."

"No, I imagine you saw all I did. But I have deduced more."

"I saw nothing remarkable except a bell-rope, but what that could mean I do not know."

"You saw the ventilator too?"

"Yes, but it is not unusual to have an opening between two rooms. It was so small that a rat could hardly pass through."

"I knew that we should find such a ventilator even before we came to Stoke Moran."

"My dear Holmes!" I exclaimed.

"Oh, yes, I did. You remember that Miss Stoner's sister complained that she could smell her stepfather's cigar. That suggested to me that there was some sort of opening between the two rooms. It had to have been a small one or the coroner would have noticed it. I deduced therefore that it was an air vent."

"But what harm can there be in that?" I asked.

"Well, there is at least a curious coincidence of dates. A ventilator is made, a bell-rope is hung, and a young lady dies. Doesn't that strike you as odd?"

"I cannot see any connection between the three things."

"Did you observe anything peculiar about the bed?" Sherlock asked.

"No."

"It was clamped to the floor. Did you ever see a bed fastened to the floor before?"

"I cannot say that I have," I answered.

"The lady could not move her bed. It obviously had to remain a certain distance away from the ventilator and the rope. I call it a rope because that is actually what it is, since no bell is attached."

"Holmes, I begin to see what you are hinting at. We are only just in time to prevent some horrible crime."

"Yes, when a doctor goes wrong he is the worst of criminals. He has nerve and he has knowledge. We shall see horrors before this night is through. For goodness sake let us smoke a quiet pipe and turn our minds to something cheerful."

At nine o'clock the light among the trees was turned out. All was dark in the direction of the Manor house. Two hours passed slowly. Then just at the stroke of eleven, a single light shone out in front of us.

"That is our signal," said Holmes springing to his feet. "It comes from the middle window."

We left the inn and went out into the dark night. A chill wind blew in our faces. The yellow light guided us through the gloom.

We walked across the grounds, and onto the lawn. We were just about to climb into the middle window when we saw a strange creature. It looked like some hideous child. It threw itself onto the lawn and then ran swiftly into the darkness.

"My God!" I whispered. "Did you see that?"

Holmes was as startled as I. Then he broke into a low laugh and said into my ear:

"That's the baboon!"

I had forgotten the strange pets the Doctor kept. There was a cheetah too. Perhaps we might find it on our shoulders any moment. We took off our shoes and climbed into the room. My friend noiselessly closed the shutters, moved the lamp onto the table, and cast his eyes around the room. All was as it had been during the day. Then he creeped up to me and whispered, "The least sound would ruin our plans."

I nodded to show that I had heard.

"We must sit without light. He would see it through the ventilator. Do not fall asleep," he whispered. "Your very life depends on it. Have your pistol ready in case we need it. I will sit on the side of the bed. You sit in that chair."

I took out my revolver and laid it on the corner of the table.

Holmes had brought a long thin cane. This he placed on the bed beside him. By it he laid a box of matches and a stump of candle. Then he turned down the lamp.

I shall never forget that night. I could not hear a sound, but I knew my friend sat wide-eyed waiting for something to happen. The shutters cut off all outside light. We were in absolute darkness. Once in a while we heard a catlike whine. It was the cheetah on the prowl. Far away we could hear the parish clock. It boomed out every quarter of an hour. Twelve struck, then one, and two, and three, and still we sat waiting.

Suddenly there was a fleeting gleam from the room next door. It vanished immediately. In its place came the smell of burning oil and heated metal. Someone in the next room had lit a lantern. I heard some movement and then all was silent once more. For half an hour I sat straining my ears. Then suddenly I heard another sound ... a gentle, soothing sound like steam escaping a tea kettle. The instant we heard it Holmes sprang from the bed, struck a match and lashed furiously with his cane at the bell-pull.

"Did you see it, Watson?" he yelled. "Did you see it?"

But I saw nothing. At the moment when Holmes struck the match I heard a low clear whistle. The sudden glare made it impossible for me to see what my friend was lashing out at. Sherlock's face had turned deathly pale. It was filled with horror and hate.

He had stopped striking the bell-pull and was now staring at the ventilator. Suddenly there was a horrible cry. It grew louder and louder. It was a yell of fear, pain, and anger. It struck cold in our hearts. I stood gazing at Holmes and he at me, until the last echoes of it had died away into the silence.

"What can it mean?" I gasped.

"It means that it is all over," answered Holmes. "And perhaps, it is for the best. Take your pistol and we shall enter Dr. Roylott's room."

He lit the lamp and led the way down the corridor. He knocked at the door twice. There came no reply. Then he turned the handle and entered. I followed with the cocked pistol in my hand.

On the table stood a lantern. Its shutter was half open. Beside the table on a wooden chair sat Dr. Grimesby Roylott. He was dressed in a long gray

dressing gown. His whip lay across his lap. His chin was cocked upward and his eyes were fixed in a dreadful stare. Around his brow he had a peculiar yellow band with brownish speckles. It seemed tightly bound around his head. Roylott made neither sound nor motion as we entered the room.

"The band! The speckled band!" whispered Holmes.

I took a step forward. In an instant his strange headgear began to move. The diamond-shaped head and puffed neck of a snake appeared.

"It's a swamp adder!" cried Holmes. "The deadliest snake in India. It has turned on its master. Let us thrust this creature back into its den. We can then take Miss Stoner to a place of shelter and let the county police know what has happened."

He took the whip swiftly from the dead man's lap and threw the noose around the reptile's neck. He lifted it from its horrid perch and carried it at arm's length to the iron safe. He threw it into the safe and closed the door firmly upon it.

Such are the true facts of Dr. Grimesby Roylott's death. The next morning we sent Miss Stoner by train to her aunt's and turned the entire matter into the hands of the local police.

"I had," said Holmes on the way back to London, "come to an entirely wrong conclusion about this case. It just goes to show that one must never make judgments without enough information. The presence of the gypsies and the use of the word 'band,' which could refer to a group of people, put me on the wrong scent. But I soon saw the error of my reasoning. There was simply no way that a human being could enter that room by the window or door. Then I spotted the fake bell-pull and the ventilator. The discovery that the bed was clamped to the floor was of key importance. It made me suspect that the rope was used as a bridge for something to pass from the ventilator opening to the bed. The idea of a snake instantly came to me. The fact that the Doctor kept creatures from India made me believe that I was on the right track. Furthermore, snake poison is very difficult to discover by chemical testing ... and it works quickly. This would appeal to the Doctor. Two little fang marks would be very hard to detect. Then I thought of the whistle. He had obviously trained it, probably by the use of the milk we saw, to return to him when he whistled. He would put the snake through the ventilator at the hour that he thought best. It would then crawl through the ventilator, along the rope and down onto the bed. It might or might not bite the occupant. Perhaps she would escape its bite every night for a week. But sooner or later he would attack.

"I had come to these conclusions before we entered his room. An inspection of his chair confirmed my thought. It showed that he had been standing on it—which of course he would have to do to reach the ventilator. The sight of the safe, the saucer of milk, and the loop in the whip decided the matter. The metallic clang that Miss Stoner heard was caused by her father hastily closing the door of his safe upon the deadly snake. Once I made up my mind, I arranged for Miss Stoner to leave her room and for us to be there in her place. When I heard the creature hiss, I instantly lit the light and attacked it."

"Which made it return through the ventilator," I added.

"Yes, and caused it to turn upon its master on the other side. You see, my blows roused its snakish temper. It flew upon the first person it saw. In a way, I am responsible for Dr. Roylott's death. In all honesty, I doubt that I shall lose much sleep because of it."

BOOK ONE

Sir Arthur Conan Doyle's
THE ADVENTURES OF
SHERLOCK HOLMES

Adapted for young readers by Catherine Edwards Sadler

Whose footsteps are those on the stairs of 221-B Baker Street, home of Mr. Sherlock Holmes, the world's greatest detective? And what incredible mysteries will challenge the wits of the genius sleuth this time?

A Study In Scarlet In the first Sherlock Holmes story ever written, Holmes and Watson embark on their first case together—an intriguing murder mystery.
The Red-headed League Holmes comes to the rescue in a most unusual heist!
The Man With The Twisted Lip Is this a case of murder, kidnapping, or something totally unexpected?

Join the uncanny and extraordinary Sherlock Holmes, and his friend and chronicler, Dr. Watson as they tackle dangerous crimes and untangle the most intricate mysteries.

AVON **C** CAMELOT

BOOK THREE

Sir Arthur Conan Doyle's

THE ADVENTURES OF
SHERLOCK HOLMES

Adapted for young readers by Catherine Edwards Sadler

The Adventure of the Engineer's Thumb When a young engineer arrives in Dr. Watson's office with his thumb missing, it leads to a mystery in a secret mansion, and a ring of deadly criminals.

The Adventure of the Beryl Coronet Holmes is sure that an accused jewel thief is innocent, but will he be able to prove it?

The Adventure of Silver Blaze Where is Silver Blaze, a favored racehorse which has vanished before a big race?

The Adventure of the Musgrave Ritual A family ritual handed down from generation to generation seemed to be mere mumbo-jumbo—until a butler disappears and a house maid goes mad.

Join the uncanny and extraordinary Sherlock Holmes, and his friend and chronicler, Dr. Watson, as they tackle dangerous crimes and untangle the most intricate mysteries.

AVON CAMELOT

AN AVON CAMELOT ORIGINAL • 78105 • $1.95
(ISBN: 0-380-78105-0)

BOOK FOUR

Sir Arthur Conan Doyle's
THE ADVENTURES OF
SHERLOCK HOLMES

Adapted for young readers by Catherine Edwards Sadler

The Adventure of the Reigate Puzzle Holmes comes near death to unravel a devilish case of murder and blackmail.

The Adventure of the Crooked Man The key to this strange mystery lies in the deadly secrets of a wicked man's past.

The Adventure of the Greek Interpreter Sherlock's brilliant older brother joins Holmes on the hunt for a bunch of ruthless villains in a case of kidnapping.

The Adventure of the Naval Treaty Only Holmes can untangle a case that threatens the national security of England, and becomes a matter of life and death.

Join the uncanny and extraordinary Sherlock Holmes, and his friend and chronicler Dr. Watson, as they tackle dangerous crimes and untangle the most intricate mysteries.

AVON CAMELOT

AN AVON CAMELOT ORIGINAL • 78113 • $1.95
(ISBN: 0-380-78113-1)